Peronel's Magic Polish

...and other stories

D1386402

ℬℬ Bounty
Books

Published in 2014 by Bounty Books,
a division of Octopus Publishing Group Ltd,
Endeavour House,
189 Shaftesbury Avenue,
London WC2H 8JY
www.octopusbooks.co.uk

An Hachette UK Company
www.hachette.co.uk
Enid Blyton ® Text copyright © 2014 Hodder & Stoughton Ltd.
Illustrations copyright © 2014 Octopus Publishing Group Ltd.
Layout copyright © 2014 Octopus Publishing Group Ltd.

Illustrated by Sara Silcock.

ISBN: 978-0-75372-650-1

A CIP catalogue record for this book is available from the
British Library.

Printed and bound by CPI Group (UK) Ltd, Croydon, CR0 4YY

CONTENTS

Peronel's
Magic Polish

Once upon a time there was a little fairy called Peronel. He lived in the King of Fairyland's palace, and his work was to clean all the brass that the head footman brought into the kitchen.

He was very good at this. He would sit all morning, and rub and polish away till the brass fire-irons and trays shone beautifully.

"That's very nice, Peronel," the cook would say to him every morning.

This made him very happy, and he beamed with pride. He thought that no one had ever polished brass as beautifully as he did.

One day, as Peronel sat polishing a brass coal bucket, he had a great idea.

"I know what I'll do!" he said. "I'll

5

invent a new polish that will make everything twice as dazzling as before! I think I know just where to find the right ingredients. How delighted everyone will be!"

So that night he slipped out into the woods and gathered roots and leaves, and a magic flower that only blossomed at midnight, and two cobwebs just newly made. Then he went back to bed.

Next day he boiled everything together, strained it through the cook's sieve, and left it to cool. Then he went to the

Wizened Witch, and asked her to sell him a little pot with a brightness spell inside. She told him:

"Empty this into your mixture at sunset, stir it well and sing these words:

Now the magic has begun,
Polish brighter than the sun!

"Then everything you polish will be brighter than it ever was before!"

"Oh, thank you!" cried Peronel, and ran happily off clutching the little pot, after paying the Wizened Witch a bright new penny he had polished the day before.

When the sun sank slowly down in the sky, Peronel fetched his jar of polish. He emptied the witch's spell of brightness into it, stirred it, and sang:

Now the magic has begun,
Polish brighter than the sun!

Next morning Peronel proudly put the polish he had made on the kitchen table, and started work. He had six brass candlesticks to clean and a table lamp. He worked very hard indeed for a whole hour until the cook came into the kitchen. She stopped and threw up her hands in great surprise.

"My goodness, Peronel!" she cried in astonishment. "What have you been doing to those candlesticks! I can hardly look at them, they're so bright!"

"I'm using a magic polish, you see," said Peronel proudly. "Isn't it lovely! I made it all myself!"

The cook called the footmen and the ladies' maids and the butler, to see what a wonderful job Peronel had done.

"Look how bright Peronel has made the candlesticks!" she said. "Isn't he clever? He's made up a magic polish of his own!"

Everybody thought Peronel was certainly very clever indeed, and the little fairy was delighted. But he longed to do something that would make the King and Queen notice him too.

You'd never guess what he did!

He fetched the King's golden crown in the middle of the night, and gave it a tremendous polishing with his magic polish! Then he quietly put it back again.

In the morning the King couldn't make out what had happened to his gleaming crown.

"It's so bright I can't bear to look at it," he said to the Queen. "It shines like the sun!"

"Put it on, then your eyes won't be dazzled," said the Queen, and the King took her advice.

But Peronel's polishing had not only made the crown bright, it had made it terribly slippery too, and it wouldn't stay straight. It kept slipping, first over one ear, then over the other, and everybody in court began to giggle.

The King became quite cross.

"Well, I don't know who's been polishing my crown," he said, "but, anyway, I wish they wouldn't! It's a silly idea!"

Peronel was just nearby, and heard what the King said. Instead of being a sensible little fairy, and deciding not to try to make people praise him any more, he became quite angry.

"All right," he thought. "I'll polish something else tonight! Nobody will know who's done it, and I'll have a bit of fun!"

So the naughty little fairy took his polish and his cloth into the King's breakfast room that night, and began polishing the gold chairs with all his might.

You can imagine what happened next

morning! The King and Queen, the Princess and the Prince, all sat down to breakfast, but they couldn't sit still! They slid and slipped and slithered about on their chairs till the footmen standing behind nearly burst themselves with trying not to laugh!

When the King disappeared under the table, everybody thought it was very funny, even the Queen.

"Dear, dear, dear!" she said, laughing. "I never saw you disappear so quickly before! I really think we'd better sit on some other chairs until the polish has worn off! Goodness knows who has made them so shiny and slippery!"

"I'll soon find out!" said the King crossly, looking very red in the face as he sat down on another chair.

"No, no, dear," said the Queen. "It was only an accident! Somebody's been doing his work too well!"

When Peronel heard what had happened, he was very pleased, and chuckled loudly. He wished he had seen it all.

"I'd like to polish something and see what happens myself," he thought. "Now, what can I polish? I know! There's a dance tomorrow night in the ballroom. I'll ask if I can help to polish the floor, and then I'll hide behind a curtain and watch all the people slipping about!"

The naughty little fairy found it was quite easy to get permission to help. The other servants were only too glad to have him, for they all knew how quick and clever he was.

While they were at lunch, he mixed a little of his magic polish into all their pots, and then ran in to his own lunch.

All afternoon Peronel and the other servants polished the floor in preparation for the dance, until it shone like sunlight.

"Dear me!" said the butler, peeping in. "You have all worked well!"

He came into the big room – and suddenly his legs slid from beneath him, and he sat down on the floor with a bump.

"Good gracious!" he cried. "Isn't the floor slippery!"

Peronel chuckled. Then he darted behind a curtain, waiting for the evening, when the guests would come in and dance.

At last they came, chattering and laughing. But, directly they began to dance on the slippery floor, their feet

didn't seem to belong to them! They went slithering everywhere – then *bumpity-bump*, the guests began tumbling down, as if they were dancing on ice!

Just then the King came into the ballroom, and stared in the greatest astonishment. Half the dancers were on the floor! "What is the matter?" he cried, striding forward.

He soon knew – for his feet flew from under him, and *bump*! – he sat down suddenly.

"Who has polished the floor like this?" he thundered. "It's as slippery as ice. Fetch the servants. I shall punish them!"

Peronel trembled behind the curtain, and wondered what he should do. He wasn't a coward, and he knew he couldn't let the servants be punished for something that was his fault.

So, to the King's surprise, Peronel rushed out from behind the curtain, and ran up to where His Majesty still sat on the floor. But he forgot that it was slippery, and he suddenly slipped, turned head-over-heels, and landed right in the King's lap!

"Bless my buttons!" roared the King in fright. "Whatever's happened now?"

Very frightened indeed, Peronel got up

off the King's lap and stood trembling
as he confessed what he had done.

"It wasn't the other servants' fault; it
was mine," he said. "And it was I who
polished your crown the other day, but I
only meant to be useful, truly I did!"

"You're a great deal too useful," the
King said crossly, getting up very
carefully. "You can choose your own
punishment, Peronel. You can either stay
in the palace and never polish anything
again, or leave the palace and take your
wonderful polish with you."

Sadly, Peronel wondered what to do.

"I don't want to do anything else but polish," he said at last. "So I'm afraid I'll have to leave the palace and take my magic polish with me."

And he did, and what do you suppose he does with it now?

He goes to the fields and meadows and polishes every single golden yellow buttercup that he finds. Look inside one, and you'll see how beautifully he does it! He misses his friends at the palace, but now he has made new friends with all the little creatures of the countryside, and he spends his days happily polishing to his heart's content!

Good Little Clockwork Mouse

The clockwork mouse loved the little doll's-house in the playroom. He often used to go and peep in at the windows and wished he could walk in at the front door.

"I'm quite small enough to," he told Mandy, who was the mother-doll in the doll's-house. "Do let me come in, Mandy. I'd so like to see all the rooms. And oh, how I'd like to sleep in one of the little beds!"

"Well, you can't," said Mandy. "This is a house for tiny dolls, not silly little clockwork mice. Go away – and if you peep in at the window again I'll smack your little nose!"

So the clockwork mouse kept away from the doll's-house except when Mandy and the other little dolls went for a walk. Then he ran to peep in at the windows again, looking longingly in at the tiny rooms. "Just big enough for me!" he said. "Oh, I do wish I could go inside."

Now one day Mandy put on her best brooch, her best hat, and her best shoes, and went out of the doll's-house to visit Angela, the golden-haired doll, who sat in her little chair at the other side of the playroom. Angela seemed like a giant to her, and Mandy always felt very grand when she could sit near her and talk to her.

"That's a very nice brooch you have on, Mandy," said Angela. "Where did you get it?"

"It came out of a cracker," Mandy said proudly. "I'll take it off and you can look at it."

But as Angela was looking at it she dropped it – and, goodness me, a small mouse who was peeping out of a nearby hole saw it and ran to it. A beautiful brooch! Ah, he would like that! He pounced on it and ran back to his hole with it before Mandy could stop him!

"My brooch! My beautiful cracker brooch!" she cried. "Bring it back, you bad little mouse!"

But the mouse wouldn't, of course. It was a treasure to him, something that glittered and gleamed and shone, and lit up his dark hole!

Mandy began to cry, and the big doll Angela was very upset. "Don't cry!" she said. "We'll send someone down the hole for your brooch. One of the toys will go."

"There's nobody small enough," wept Mandy. "I know the brave teddy bear

would go if he could – but he'd never squeeze into that hole!"

The little clockwork mouse ran up. "Mandy, I'll get it for you," he said. "I'm as small as any real mouse. I can easily squeeze into the hole!"

"Aren't you afraid?" asked Mandy. "There might be dozens of mice down there – they might fight you and bite you."

"Well – I am a bit afraid," said the clockwork mouse. "But I know how proud you are of your brooch, Mandy – and it really is very beautiful. I'll go down

the hole and see if I can get it back."

And down the hole he went! He soon came to where the little family of mice lived, and they were most surprised to see him. He was quite fierce with them.

"Now then, now then – what do you mean by stealing Mandy's brooch?" he said. "I can tell you it's a very good thing that I came to get it – and not the big teddy bear, or the clown or the tin soldiers! My word, you wouldn't like them to march down here with their swords, would you?"

The mice were frightened. Goodness – soldiers marching down their hole! What a dreadful thought!

"Here – take the brooch quickly!" said the little mouse who had stolen it. "Say I am sorry – and please don't let the teddy bear or the clown or the soldiers come down here."

The clockwork mouse took the brooch in his mouth and ran back up the hole. He dropped the brooch at Mandy's feet.

"You dear, kind, brave little mouse," she said, and she kissed him on the nose. "I'm sorry I wouldn't let you come into my doll's-house. Please do come now whenever you like, and once a week you can sleep in one of the little beds!"

So now when the toys miss the clockwork mouse they always know where he is – playing in the doll's-house, or fast asleep in one of their tiny beds!

Mr Grumpygroo's Hat

Mr Grumpygroo was the crossest old man in the whole of Tweedle Village. No one had ever seen him smile, or heard him laugh. He was so mean that he saved all his crumbs and made them into a pudding instead of giving them to the birds.

Of course, everyone was a little frightened of Mr Grumpygroo. They kept out of his way and the children hid if they saw him coming. He didn't seem to mind. He lived all alone in his tumble-down cottage, and made friends with no one.

But really Mr Grumpygroo was very lonely. He often wished the children would smile at him as they smiled at the other villagers. But they never did, and old Grumpygroo vowed that he wouldn't be the first to smile at anyone, not he!

Every day he went walking through the village with his old green scarf round his neck and his battered brown hat on his head, leaning heavily on his walking stick.

He might have gone on scowling and frowning for ever, if something strange hadn't happened. One morning he went into the hall to fetch his scarf and his hat. It was rather a dark day, and Mr Grumpygroo could hardly see. He felt about for his scarf, and tied it round his neck. Then he groped about for his hat.

There was a lamp standing in the hall on the old chest where Mr Grumpygroo usually stood his hat. On it was a lampshade made of yellow silk with a fringe of coloured beads. By mistake Mr Grumpygroo took up the shade instead of his hat, and it was so dark that he didn't see the mistake he had made. He put the lampshade on his head! It felt rather like his old brown battered hat, so he didn't notice any difference; and out he walked into the street.

He looked very funny indeed, walking along with a lampshade on his head. All the beads shook as he walked. As he went out of his gate the sun came out, the birds began to sing, and it turned into a lovely spring day.

Even old Mr Grumpygroo felt a little bit glad, and he half wished he had a friend who would smile at him. But he knew nobody would, so he set his face into a scowl, and went down the street.

The first person he met was the jolly balloon woman carrying her load of balloons. When she saw the yellow

lampshade on his head, she smiled, for he looked so very funny.

Mr Grumpygroo thought she was smiling at him, as he didn't know what he had on his head, and he was most surprised. He didn't smile back, but went on his way, wondering why the balloon woman had looked so friendly for the first time in ten years.

The next person he met was Mr Plod, the village policeman, who loved a joke. When he saw the lampshade perched on old Mr Grumpygroo's head, he grinned very broadly indeed.

Mr Grumpygroo blinked in surprise. Could it be the fine spring morning that was making people so friendly?

"I shall smile back at the very next person who smiles at me," said old Mr Grumpygroo to himself, feeling quite excited. "If people are going to be friendly, I don't mind being nice too."

Round the corner he met Mr Macdonald the farmer riding on his old horse. As soon as the farmer caught sight of the lampshade, he smiled so widely that his mouth almost reached his ears.

And so Mr Grumpygroo smiled back! Old Macdonald nearly fell off his horse with astonishment, for he had never seen such a thing before! He ambled on, lost in surprise, and Mr Gumpygroo went on his way with a funny warm feeling round his heart.

"I've smiled at someone!" he said to himself. "I've forgotten how nice it was. I hope someone else smiles at me, for I wouldn't mind doing it a second time."

Four little children came running up the street. As soon as they saw Mr

Grumpygroo with the yellow lampshade on his head, they forgot to run and hide as they usually did. Instead, they smiled and laughed in delight.

Mr Grumpygroo was so pleased. He smiled too, and the ice round his heart melted a little bit more. He was starting to enjoy this strange new feeling.

The children laughed merrily and one of them put her hand in his, for she thought that Mr Grumpygroo had put the lampshade on to amuse her.

Something funny happened inside Mr Grumpygroo then. He wanted to sing and dance. It was lovely to have people so friendly towards him.

The next person he met was Mr Crumb, the baker. Mr Grumpygroo smiled at him before Mr Crumb had time to smile first. The baker was so surprised that he nearly dropped the load of new-made cakes he was carrying. Then he saw Mr Grumpygroo's lampshade hat, and he gave a deep chuckle. Mr Grumpygroo was delighted to see him being so friendly.

"Good morning," he said to Mr Crumb. "It's a wonderful day, isn't it?"

The baker nodded his head and laughed again.

"Yes," he said, "and that's a wonderful hat you're wearing, Mr Grumpygroo."

Mr Grumpygroo went on, very pleased. "What a nice fellow to admire my old hat," he thought. "Dear me, and I always thought the people of this village were so unpleasant. That just shows how mistaken I can be!"

He smiled at everyone he met, and everyone smiled back, wondering why Mr Grumpygroo wore such a funny thing on his head. By the time he reached home again, he was quite a different man. He smiled and hummed a little tune, and he even did a little jig when he got into his front garden. He was so happy to think that people had been friendly to him.

"It shows I can't be as grumpy and cross as they thought I was," he said to himself. "Well, well, I'll show them what a fine man I am. I'll give a grand party, and invite everyone in the village to it. Whatever will they say to that!"

He walked into his hall, and was just going to take off his hat when he saw himself in the mirror. He stood and stared in surprise – whatever had he got on his head?

"Oh my, oh my, it's the lampshade!" He groaned and took it off. "Fancy going out in that! And oh dear! Everyone smiled at the lampshade, because it looked so funny – they didn't smile at me after all!"

How upset Mr Grumpygroo was! "How dreadful to have to wear a lampshade on my head before people will smile at me!" he groaned. "I must be a most unpleasant old man. Well, I will just have to show people that I've changed. I had better organise my party right away. Perhaps the village folk will learn to smile at me for myself if I'm nice to them. I'll send out those party invitations at once!"

He did – and wasn't everybody surprised!

The party was a great success, everyone had a wonderful time and soon old Grumpygroo had heaps of friends. Nobody could imagine what had changed the old fellow and made him so nice, nor could anyone understand why he kept his old yellow lampshade so carefully on display, long after it was dirty and torn.

But Mr Grumpygroo knew why! It had brought him smiles and plenty of friends, but he wasn't going to tell anyone that – not he!

Whiskers and
the Wizard

There was once a wizard called Blunder. He was the youngest and smallest of all the wizards, and he was not very good at learning magic.

He made so many mistakes that all the other wizards laughed at him.

"One of these days you'll cast a magic spell on yourself by mistake," they said, "and then you'll be in a fine pickle!"

But Blunder wouldn't listen to any advice. He thought he knew everything.

He carried on making spells, stirring up strange recipes for magic in his boiling cauldron, and muttering enchanted words to himself. He had one servant – a faithful little rabbit called Whiskers. Most wizards, like witches, have cats for servants, for cats are wise and can keep secrets. But magic cats cost a great deal of money and Blunder couldn't afford one. So he had a rabbit instead, which was much cheaper.

Whiskers was a very clean and tidy servant. He swept and dusted, cooked and mended, and looked after Blunder very well indeed. Sometimes he stirred the cauldron himself, though he was afraid of what magic might come out of it.

When he saw that Blunder often made mistakes, he was worried in case the little wizard should harm himself. He was very fond of his master, and wouldn't

have let anything happen to him for all the world. So one day Whiskers asked if he could look at all the magic books. That way he thought he might learn some magic himself, and perhaps be able to help Blunder one day. But Blunder just laughed at him.

"Why, you're only a rabbit!" he said. "You'll never be able to learn any magic. But you can look at my magic books if you like."

So Whiskers waited until his work was done. Then he took down the magic books one by one, and read them all. He had a good memory, and very soon he knew a great many spells, and could say hundreds of magic words.

One day he saw Blunder mixing spiders' webs, blue mushrooms and the yolk from a goose's egg, chanting as he went:

> Tick-a-too, fa-la-lee,
> Tar-ra, tar-ra, tar-roo,
> Dickety, hickety, jiminy-japes,
> Bibble and scribble and boo!

36

"Master! Master!" cried Whiskers, dropping his broom in a hurry. "You're saying the wrong words! Instead of making magic to grow a goose that lays golden eggs, you are saying a spell that will turn you into a goose yourself!"

It was true! Blunder had made a mistake. Already feathers had begun to sprout from his shoulders! Hurriedly he began to chant the right spell, and the feathers slowly disappeared.

But instead of being grateful to Whiskers, he was cross with him!

"I'd soon have found out my mistake!" he said sharply. "Get on with your work, Whiskers, and in future don't interfere in things that you know nothing about."

The next day, the powerful Wizard of Woz came to tea, but he arrived with bad news.

"The wicked goblin has been seen again in Pixie Wood," said the old wizard. "So we want you to get rid of him, Blunder. Or better still, make some magic that will get him into our power. Then we can make him into a useful servant. You know how to do it, don't you?"

"Of course I do!" said Blunder. "You can trust me to do a simple thing like that! The goblin will be in your power before midnight."

Blunder set to work as soon as the wizard had gone. He mixed together green elderberries, a small moonbeam, two thorns from a blue rose, and a drop of honey. Then he had to count from ninety-nine back to one, and stir all the time from left to right.

"Ninety-nine, ninety-eight, ninety-seven," began Blunder and he had almost got to twenty, when Whiskers gave a cry of fear.

"Master! You're stirring the wrong way! Oh dear, oh dear, you'll put yourself in the goblin's power, instead of getting him into yours!"

Blunder stopped stirring in fright and began stirring the other way – but you can't do that sort of thing in the middle of a powerful spell! Something is bound to happen, and all of a sudden it did! There was a tremendous bang and a blue-green flame shot out of the cauldron and whizzed twice around the room.

Then it turned into a swirling purple wind that whisked Blunder up into the air and out of the window!

Whiskers crouched in a corner and waited for something else to happen. But nothing did – except that he heard a very strange laugh from somewhere that made him shiver and tremble.

"That was the goblin!" thought the little rabbit. "He knows that Blunder has put himself in his power, and he's come to get him. Oh dear, I must try to rescue him at once!"

Meanwhile Blunder had flown out of the window, risen as high as the clouds, and then come down, *bump*, in a place he didn't know!

"This is a fine thing!" he said. "Now what am I to do?" But at that moment he heard a nasty laugh, and suddenly there in front of him stood the wicked little goblin.

"Ho, ho!" said the goblin. "Now you're in my power, Blunder. You don't deserve to be a wizard when you make such silly mistakes. Come along, I'm going to keep you in my cave and you can be my servant!"

"Never!" cried Blunder. "I won't go."

But the goblin knew a little magic too. He muttered a few strange words, and at once Blunder's feet began to walk in the direction that the goblin wished them to.

"You will stay here until I get back," said the wicked goblin when they had reached his cave. "And just in case you try to misbehave, this will stop you."

He drew a white chalk circle right round poor Blunder, who watched him in

dismay, for he knew that the circle was a magic one and would stop him using any spells to escape.

"Please set me free," Blunder begged.

But the goblin would not listen. He just clapped his hands seven times, laughed and disappeared. At the same time a great stone rolled over the entrance to the cave, leaving Blunder all alone in the cold and dark.

"No one but Whiskers knows I am gone!" he wept. "And how will he be able to help me? He's only a silly little rabbit."

Little did Blunder know that at that very moment Whiskers was busy searching for him. He had just reached the edge of Goblinland and was trying to decide which way to go first.

"Now what I need is that spell I read the other day," muttered Whiskers to himself. "That will help me find my master."

Soon he had remembered what to do. He took five green leaves and put them in a circle with their ends touching. Then he found a white feather and blew it into

the air, singing the magic words as he did so. When he looked down again, the leaves had vanished! But the feather was still floating in front of him, floating away to the west as if blown by a strong breeze.

"Lead me to my master!" cried the rabbit, and followed the feather as it danced off down the hillside.

Soon it brought Whiskers to the cave. As soon as the little rabbit saw the great stone at the entrance he felt certain that his master was imprisoned behind it.

"Master, Master!" he called out. "Are you there? It's me, Whiskers." Inside the cave, Blunder could not believe his ears.

"Oh, Whiskers, is it really you!" he cried. "I have been trapped in here by the wicked goblin. Can you help me escape? Can you move the stone?"

But even though Whiskers pushed against the great stone with all his strength, he could not move it even the smallest amount.

"Never mind," said the little wizard, in despair. "Even if you could move it, it wouldn't be much use, for I can't move

out of this magic circle. And even if I knew how to do that, I can't remember the spell that would get rid of the goblin's power."

"Perhaps I can help," cried the little rabbit. "I think I can remember the spell about goblins." And he started to recite it carefully to Blunder.

"That's just the one I want!" cried Blunder. "Oh, Whiskers! If only you could gather all the ingredients together, I might be able to escape. But I'm afraid it's quite impossible."

"Why's that?" said Whiskers in dismay.

"Because the final ingredient is a hair from my head," explained Blunder. "So unless we can move this stone, I'm stuck. I shall have to be that horrid goblin's slave forever."

Whiskers pushed at the great stone again, but it was no use. Then he had a brilliant idea! Wasn't he a rabbit? Couldn't he burrow like all rabbits do?

At once he began to burrow into the hillside, just beside the cave entrance. He sent out the earth in great showers, and in minutes he had made a tunnel into the cave where Blunder sat.

"Hooray!" cried Blunder. "You're quite the most brilliant rabbit in the whole world. Now we can get to work."

The little wizard knew that the one thing that could destroy the goblin's power was the sight of a red frilled dragon. And the spell told them exactly how to make one. So all that day and all that night brave little Whiskers went in and out of his tunnel, fetching nightshade berries, white feathers, blue toadstools, sunbeams, moonbeams and everything else that Blunder needed.

Soon all the ingredients were neatly piled at one end of the enormous cave. Whiskers put the last one on the very top and then sat down with his master to wait for the goblin to return.

Early the next morning they heard the goblin outside the cave. He shouted a magic word, and the stone flew away from the entrance. Then he strode in. Whiskers had hidden himself, and Blunder was pretending to be asleep.

"Ho ho! Ha ha!" said the goblin. "What about a nice hot breakfast, Blunder? You must be hungry by now."

The wizard pretended to groan.

"Well, tell me a few secret spells and I will give you some toast and eggs," said the goblin.

"Here is one," said Blunder, raising his head, and he began to chant the spell that would turn all the magic things at the end of the cave into a fearful frilled dragon! The goblin listened carefully, grinning all the while because he thought that he was hearing a wonderful new spell.

Then, just as Blunder got to the last words, a strange thing happened. A rushing, swishing noise came from the end of the cave, and suddenly a dreadful bellow rang out. Then two yellow eyes gleamed, and lo and behold, a great dragon came rushing out!

"A frilled dragon!" yelled the goblin in fright. "Oh my! Oh my! A great red frilled dragon! Let me out! Let me go!"

And the goblin leaped high into the air, turned into a puff of smoke, and streamed out of the cave with the dragon after him. Whiskers and Blunder followed, and the last they saw of the wicked goblin was a thin cloud of smoke way up in the eastern sky. The dragon soon gave up the chase, and turned back towards the cave.

"Quick!" whispered Whiskers. "Change him into something else or he will eat us too!"

Blunder clapped his hands twice, and uttered a command. The dragon began to shrink, and when it was as small as a football it turned into a mass of red

flames. Whiskers hurriedly filled a jug with water and gave it to Blunder, who threw it over the flames – and *sizzle-sizzle-sizzle*, they went out! Nothing was left of the frilled dragon except for a few wet ashes.

"My goodness," said Blunder, sitting down on the ground with a sigh. "We have been having too many adventures, Whiskers. I shall be glad to get home and sleep in my soft bed!"

"Poor Master, you must be very tired," said the kind rabbit. "Jump up on my back, and I'll take you home before you can say tiddley-winks!"

So Blunder climbed up on Whiskers' soft back, and very soon he was safely home.

"Thank you very much for all you have done for me," said the little wizard, hugging the delighted rabbit. "I think you are much cleverer than I am, Whiskers. From now on you shall be my partner, not my servant, and you shall wear a pointed hat like me! We will do all our spells together, and then perhaps I shan't ever make a mistake again!"

Whiskers was so pleased.

"Well, let's go to bed now and have some sleep," said Blunder, yawning. "I can hardly keep my eyes open. Then tomorrow, we will go and buy your pointed hat." So they both fell asleep, and Whiskers dreamed happily of wearing a pointed hat and helping Blunder with his spells.

Many years have passed since Blunder had his adventure with the wicked goblin. Whiskers is still with him, but now Blunder is very old, and Whiskers' ears have gone grey with age.

Sometimes when all their work is done, they sit one on each side of the fireplace, and Whiskers says, "Do you remember that time when you made a mistake in your spells?"

Then they both laugh loudly, and wonder where the wicked goblin went to – for he has never been heard of from that day to this.

Nursery-Rhyme Land

Once upon a time there were twins called Tom and Polly. They had curly hair, rosy cheeks, and blue eyes. They were happy children, always ready for a game and a laugh. And they were always looking out for an adventure!

One day the sun shone brightly, the birds sang, and the twins thought they would go out for a walk.

"Let's go somewhere that we've never been before," said Tom. "Let's go right over the hill and down the other side. We might find an adventure!"

So off they went, running along in the sunshine. They climbed up the hill and set off down the other side. They came to a pretty lane, with white may on the hedges on each side.

"Let's go along here," said Polly. They didn't meet anyone at all.

The cows in the field looked over the hedge at them, and some sheep baa'd loudly. They could hear ducks quacking on a pond.

Just then they spotted someone coming toward them. It was a little girl, with a big crook in her hand. She was crying. Tom felt sorry for her.

"What's the matter?" he said.

"I've lost my sheep," said the little girl. "I suppose you haven't seen them, have you? There are about twenty of them."

"Well, we saw some sheep away back down the lane," said Tom. "They were baa-ing loudly. Perhaps they were yours."

"Oh, thank you," said the little girl, and hurried away, carrying her big crook. Polly turned and looked after her.

"Tom," she said suddenly, "do you know – I believe that was Little Bo-Peep!"

"Don't be silly," said Tom. "Bo-Peep's only a nursery-rhyme person. That was a real girl."

They went on down the lane and suddenly came to a place where it divided into two. A big signpost stood there. And guess what? On one of its fingers was printed in big bold letters:

TO NURSERY-RHYME LAND

"Goodness gracious!" said Polly, staring. "Look what that says, Tom. To Nursery-Rhyme Land. Then that *must* have been Little Bo-Peep. I thought it was!"

"Polly – let's go to Nursery-Rhyme Land!" said Tom, excitedly. "It would be a real adventure! Let's go!"

"All right," said Polly. "But look, there's somebody sitting down by the signpost. I hope he'll let us go by."

As they walked past the signpost, the little man who was sitting underneath it, reading a newspaper, got up. He stood in the middle of the lane and held out both his hands so that they could not get past.

"Only nursery-rhyme folk allowed this way," he said. "What are your names?"

"Mine's Tom," said Tom.

"And I'm Polly," said Polly. "Please let us pass."

"Well, I don't know which nursery-rhyme Tom you are, nor which Polly you are," said the man, "but those are nursery-rhyme names all right. You may pass. But let me warn you not to get into any trouble today, because the Old Woman Who Lives in a Shoe is in a very bad temper."

"Oh," said Polly, rather alarmed. But

Tom pulled her on, past the little man. They ran on down the lane, and came to a little village. The children sat down on the edge of an old well, and watched the people going here and there.

"I'm sure these are all nursery-rhyme people!" said Polly, feeling really excited. "Tom, doesn't that look exactly like Old Mother Hubbard? And look, she's got a dog following her – the one that was sad when the cupboard was bare."

"And isn't that Wee Willie Winkie?" said Tom, as a little boy ran past them. "He's still got his nightgown on! I suppose he always wears it!"

It really was fun watching all the people. Polly and Tom felt too shy to speak to any of them, but nobody took any notice of the twins on the well.

Suddenly a bell began to ring. It was twelve o'clock. Lunch-time! The people all hurried into their houses. *Ding-dong, ding-dong*! went the bell.

"Look," said Polly, "there's a boy coming. He's carrying a cat. He doesn't look very friendly, does he? And isn't he thin?"

"He's coming here to the well," said Tom. The boy ran up to the well and pushed the twins aside.

"Get out of my way," he said rudely, and then, to the children's horror, he dropped the cat down the well! *Splash!*

"Oh, you bad boy!" cried Polly, and leaned over to see the poor cat splashing about in the water. The boy ran off, laughing.

"That's Johnny Thin, the nasty boy who put the cat into the well, in the rhyme," said Polly, almost in tears. "Tom, what can we do?"

"Let's go and knock on the door of the nearest cottage and get help," said Tom. So he ran to a nearby cottage, and knocked loudly.

A much fatter boy came to the door, smiling. "What's the matter?" he said. "Don't tell me the cat's down the well again!"

Tom recognised him as Johnny Stout.

"Yes, it is. Do come and get it before it's drowned!" begged Tom.

Johnny ran to the well with the others. He let down the bucket and the cat climbed into it. Then Johnny Stout

wound up the bucket, and up came the cat. She at once jumped out, shook herself, and ran off.

"One of these days Johnny Thin will be caught by the Old Woman Who Lives in a Shoe!" said Johnny Stout. "She's always on the look-out for him – and for that bad Tom the Piper's Son, too. My word, when she catches them, what a telling-off they will get!"

A lovely smell came out of Johnny Stout's cottage. It made the children feel hungry. Johnny Stout noticed their hungry looks.

"Are you hungry?" he said. "I'm sorry I've no lunch to offer you, there's only the smell of it left now. But you could go over to Jack Sprat's cottage, and ask Mrs Sprat if she's got any food for you. Jack Sprat's away and there may be some meat left over. She won't eat any lean meat, you know."

Polly and Tom walked over to the trim little cottage near the green. Mrs Sprat opened the door herself.

"We're rather hungry," said Tom. "I

suppose you haven't any lunch to spare, Dame Sprat?"

"Bless your hearts, I've plenty!" said the plump old lady. "Jack Sprat's gone to market, and there's his share of the stew left. I've had mine. I pick out all the fat bits, you know, and he has all the lean ones. Come along in and eat."

They sat down and ate good helpings of a most delicious stew. Dame Sprat watched them, and then gave them some treacle tart. It was very good.

"What are your names?" she said. "I don't seem to know you – and I thought I knew everyone in this land. You must belong here, because no one is allowed in unless they are nursery-rhyme folk."

Polly and Tom turned red. They stared at the smiling old lady.

"My name's Tom," said Tom.

"What! You're surely not Tom, the Piper's Son!" cried Dame Sprat, and she looked angry. "I wouldn't have him in my house for anything, the rogue. He stole a pig, the rascal."

"No, I'm not that Tom," said Tom. "I'd never steal pigs or do things like that."

"Well, you must be Tommy Tucker, then!" said Dame Sprat. "Stand up and let me hear you sing! You sing for your supper, so you can sing for that large meal you've had!"

"I can't sing," said Tom, and he turned red. "I go all out of tune. But Polly here sings nicely."

"Polly! Are you naughty little Polly Flinders?" asked Dame Sprat. "Well, all I can say is I hope your mother punishes you if you go and sit in the cinders again! You two had better go home. I'm sure your mothers must be looking for you!"

Polly and Tom ran out, quite glad to get away from Dame Sprat's questions. They ran into a little wood that lay at the back of the village. Polly sat down on the grass. Then she pointed to something.

"Look, Tom," she said. "Someone has upset some milk and left it here with the bowl and spoon."

"Well – that must be Little Miss Muffet then," said Tom. "We'd better look out for the spider!"

Just as he spoke, something dropped from a nearby tree, hanging on a silken thread. It was the biggest spider the children had ever seen in their lives!

The twins were not afraid of ordinary spiders – but this one was too big! It looked at them out of its eight eyes, and it waved eight hairy legs in the air.

"Polly, run!" said Tom, and they ran. They bumped into a little girl hiding behind a tree. It was Little Miss Muffet.

"Has the spider gone?" asked Miss Muffet. "I want to get my bowl and spoon. Oh no, there it is! Run!"

They all ran through the wood. They came at last to a road, and coming down it they saw soldiers riding on horses, with flags waving, looking very colourful.

"There go all the King's horses and all the King's men," said Miss Muffet.

"And there's Humpty Dumpty!" cried Polly, pointing to a large, egg-shaped person sitting on a wall. "I hope he won't fall!"

"He always does," said Miss Muffet. "He loves to give the soldiers a fright. There he goes, look! All broken into pieces, as usual!"

The horses reared up as Humpty Dumpty fell. Some of the soldiers tumbled off. Others ran to Humpty Dumpty, but they couldn't possibly mend him.

"He's stupid," said Miss Muffet. "He'll have to wait until Old Mother Hubbard comes by, now. She's the only one who can mend him. She knows a powerful spell."

The twins left Miss Muffet and followed the soldiers, trotting down the

road. Soon they came to a palace. From inside there came the sound of fiddles playing a merry tune.

"Old King Cole has got his fiddlers three today," said one soldier to another. "Would you like to see him, children? He likes visitors."

Polly and Tom longed to go into the palace, of course, and see Old King Cole. So in they went, up a long, long flight of steps. Inside was an enormous hall, down the middle of which ran a large table. A meal was laid on the table, and Old King Cole was just about to seat himself at the head. Three fiddlers stood near him, playing merrily.

"Hello, hello!" he cried, as he saw the children. "Visitors! Splendid! Sit down, my dears, sit down. There's a pie coming in. Now, just let me see if I've got sixpence for you!"

He put his hand into his pocket and brought out a shiny sixpence. He gave it to Polly. Then he put his hand into his other pocket – and brought out a handful of rye seeds! He threw them down crossly.

"I've got my pocket full of rye again! Most annoying! Who puts it there, I'd like to know? Ah, here comes the pie, Good, I'm hungry. I hope it's a rabbit-pie!"

By this time the twins knew quite well what the enormous pie would be! Polly whispered to Tom:

"Sing a song of sixpence, a pocket full of rye, four and twenty blackbirds ..."

"Stop whispering!" said Old King Cole. "Now – I'll give you a piece of this lovely pie!" He took up a large knife, and Polly called to him:

"Stop, Your Majesty! There are twenty-four blackbirds in that pie!"

"Nonsense!" said the King, and he put his knife into the crust. At once there came the flutter of many wings, and the flute-like whistle of blackbirds! And out of the enormous pie flew four and twenty blackbirds! They went to the window and flew out at the top. The King sat back in astonishment.

"Now, I won't have tricks like this played on me!" he cried. "Where's the Queen? Fetch her at once!"

Nobody seemed to know where she was. Polly spoke up.

"She's in the parlour, eating bread and honey," she said. "Perhaps she knew it was only a blackbird pie, and thought she would rather have something else."

There came a sudden scream from the garden. Old King Cole jumped in alarm.

"That will be the blackbirds trying to peck off your maid's nose," said Polly.

Old King Cole banged angrily on the table.

"Who are these children who seem to know so much?" he roared. "Blackbirds in my pie! The Queen eating bread and honey! Birds pecking my maid's nose! What next I should like to know! Bring me my pipe and my bowl and take these children to prison!"

Polly and Tom each gave a loud scream.

"Quick, Polly, run!" cried Tom, and took his sister's hand. The soldiers barred

the way to the great front entrance of the palace, so the children ran to another door. This led to the kitchens. They ran through them and out into the palace garden. The maid was sitting down there crying and rubbing her nose.

Down the garden path went the children and out of a gate in the palace wall. They didn't stop running until they were too out of breath to run any more. Then they sat down on a little hillside. Polly panted and Tom puffed. They both kept a sharp look-out for the soldiers.

After they had rested for a while, Tom and Polly went down the road again, wondering what was going to happen next! Really, it was very exciting to meet so many people they had only known before in their nursery rhymes.

A boy came running toward them. He looked frightened. He carried a fiddle in his hands, and tears were running down his cheeks.

"Oh!" he called, when he saw Tom and Polly. "Save me, save me!"

"What from?" asked Polly.

"From the farmer!" cried the boy. "I'm Tom the Piper's Son, and ever since I stole a pig from the farmer, he watches out for me and beats me when he catches me. I was just playing my fiddle in the market to get a few pennies when he saw me. There he comes now! Hold my fiddle for me, will you?"

He tossed Tom his fiddle and ran on, howling. A fat farmer appeared round the corner, glared at Tom and Polly, and went puffing after the other boy.

"What am I supposed to do with his

fiddle?" said Tom, laughing. "Let's go on to the market, shall we? It sounds exciting. Tom the Piper's Son may come back there, and find us to get back his fiddle."

They walked on and came to the market. Bo-Peep was there with her sheep. Little Boy Blue was there with his horn, telling everyone how he had fallen asleep again that day and let the sheep into the meadow and the cow into the corn.

Suddenly a cat walked up on its hind legs, with a little dog. He spoke sharply to Tom.

"Where did you get that fiddle? I believe it's mine."

"No, it's not," said Polly. "And don't talk to Tom like that."

"Ho! So it's Tom the Piper's Son, who learned to play when he was young, is it?" cried the farmer's wife, who suddenly appeared behind them. "Why, my husband has just gone after him. Didn't he steal a pig of ours and eat it? Yes, he did, the scamp."

"I tell you I'm not Tom the Piper's Son," said Tom.

"Well, there's only one other Tom in Nursery-Rhyme Land, and that's Tommy Tucker," said the farmer's wife. "Sing and show us you are Tommy Tucker."

"I'm not Tommy Tucker, either," said Tom. "And this fiddle doesn't belong to that cat. Tom the Piper's Son gave it to me to hold."

"It *is* my fiddle!" said the cat. "I used it last night, when the cow jumped over the moon. Then the dish ran away with the spoon, and now there's only me and the little dog left. I put my fiddle under a bush and this morning it was gone. You must have taken it. Shame on you! Who are you, anyway?"

"I'm Tom and she's Polly," said Tom, beginning to be frightened, because by now quite a crowd had collected around them. "We only came here for an adventure. We don't really belong. We'd better go home."

"They don't belong!" cried everyone. "They don't belong. What shall we do with them?"

Up came an old woman wearing a big bonnet and a shawl. "I'll take them," she said. "I know what to do with naughty children. There's plenty of room in my shoe!"

Polly gave a squeal.

"I don't want to go with you!" she cried. But the Old Woman had them firmly by the hand. She led them across the market, kicking and struggling. She went down a little street and they came to a field. In the field was the shoe!

But what an enormous one! It must surely have belonged to a giant, for it

was big enough to take at least twenty
children! A roof had been built over it,
with a chimney. There was a door in one
side, and windows too. Many children
were playing about in the field outside
the shoe.

"Oh, he's got a fiddle!" cried one little
girl. "You must be Tom the Piper's Son.
I knew the Old Woman would get you
some day. Play to us!"

Crash! One of the windows in the house was suddenly smashed. It made Tom and Polly jump. The Old Woman turned and looked at the suddenly quiet children.

"Who threw that stone?" she said. Nobody answered. The Old Woman was very angry. "That's the third time this week that window has been broken. Indoors all of you!"

The frightened children ran into the strange shoe house. Tom and Polly went with them. The Old Woman followed, and shut the door with a bang. Polly whispered the rhyme to Tom:

> There was an old woman
> Who lived in a shoe;
> She had so many children
> She didn't know what to do;
> She gave them some broth
> Without any bread,
> And whipped them all soundly
> And put them to bed.

"It isn't fair that we should be kept

here," whispered Polly. "I don't want to be whipped and sent to bed. Look – let's run out of the back door."

Tom and Polly dashed out. The Old Woman jumped up and ran after them, but they had a very good start. They ran quickly across the field, as fast as their legs would take them. They went through a gate and out into a lane. They saw a stile and climbed over it. Beyond was a cornfield, and Polly saw Little Boy Blue's cow still in the corn.

They took the path and ran across to a little wood. The Old Woman was still after them, and behind her streamed all the children, yelling loudly. Into the wood

went Polly and Tom, and soon found a path to follow. After a bit the Old Woman and her children could no longer be heard.

"We're safe," said Polly. "But how are we to get home, Tom? We're quite lost!"

"No, we're not!" said Tom, as he looked around. "Why, this is the wood near our house. We shall soon be home."

"So it is!" cried Polly. "Oh, Tom, whatever will people say when we tell them about our adventure!"

"Nobody will believe us," said Tom. "Nobody! I wonder if it could have been a dream. Do you think it was, Polly?"

"Well, if you still have Tom the Piper's Son's fiddle when we get home, and I have my sixpence, it couldn't be a dream," said Polly.

They were soon home and safe in the kitchen. They looked at one another.

"I've still got the fiddle – and if Tom doesn't come to fetch it, I'm going to learn to play it!" said Tom.

"And I have my sixpence, so it really did happen, Tom. We've been to Nursery-

Rhyme Land after all. What an exciting time we've had!"

They had, hadn't they? Look out for the signpost on your walks, if you want to go there, too. But beware of the Old Woman in the Shoe.

Smokey and
the Seagull

"I wish my mistress wouldn't put my dinner out of doors," said Smokey the cat to his friend Sooty. Smokey was on the wall with him, and their long tails hung down, twitching just a little.

"Why? What does it matter if she does?" said Sooty. "It tastes just the same, indoors or out!"

"I know. But there's a big seagull that comes in from the beach," said Smokey, "and he sits on our roof and watches for my mistress to come out with my dinner – it's always a nice bit of fish, you know, and that seagull loves fish! And as soon as he sees my mistress coming out with my dish, down he flies to it and gobbles up my dinner!"

"Well, I wonder you allow that!" said

81

Sooty, swinging his black tail angrily as he thought of the greedy seagull. "I have my dinner indoors, thank goodness!"

"My mistress won't let me have it there," said Smokey, mournfully. "She says I make too much mess. So what am I to do?"

"Pounce on the seagull, of course," said Sooty. "That's easy."

"Sooty – have you ever seen a seagull close to?" asked Smokey. "Do you know how big it is?"

"No, I never go down on the beach," said Sooty. "I don't like walking in soft sand – it's like snow, and my paws sink right down."

"Well – a seagull is enormous," said Smokey. "I wouldn't dare to pounce on it."

"Well, just pounce on its tail, then," said Sooty. "And hang on for all you are worth. Pull out a few feathers if you can – then that seagull won't come again!"

"Yes, that may be quite a good idea," said Smokey. "It is its beak I'm scared of – it's so big and strong. I really believe it could bite off my tail!"

"Well, you get hold of the seagull's tail first!" said Sooty. "I'll sit up here and cheer you on. Do be brave, Smokey."

"That's all very well," said Smokey. "You'd think twice before you pounced on a great seagull! Still, I'll try it. I'll hide behind the dustbin and wait till the gull comes down. Then, when it has its back to me, I'll pounce!"

"What time do you have your dinner?" asked Sooty. "I really must watch this."

"When that big clock over there strikes one," said Smokey. "Mistress comes out just after that. Sooty, will you come to my help if I need it?"

"Of course. Certainly!" said Sooty. "I'll leap right on top of the gull and bite his neck!"

"You are brave!" said Smokey, admiringly. "All right – watch out for my mistress to come at dinner-time."

He jumped down from the wall and ran off to the house. Just before he went indoors he looked up at the sky. There were the big seagulls, gliding to and fro on the breeze, their enormous wings spread wide. Smokey wondered which of them was the one that stole his dinner!

He smelled his fish cooking on the kitchen stove and felt hungry. Yesterday the seagull had gobbled all his dinner up, and poor Smokey had only been able to lick out the dish. How he hoped he would be able to eat it all himself today!

"Are you hungry, little cat?" asked his mistress. "Well, you shall have your fish as soon as it is cool. Don't keep walking round my legs like that – it won't make your dinner come any quicker!"

When the big clock struck one, Sooty
jumped up on the wall to see if Smokey
really did mean to pounce on the seagull. He saw his friend come running out
of the house and then he hid behind the
dustbin. Only the tip of his whiskers
could be seen.

Overhead a big gull spread its white
wings and waited for Smokey's dinner
to arrive!

Sooty gazed up at it and felt quite
scared when he saw how big it was.

Goodness – would Smokey be brave enough to pounce on that enormous bird?

Smokey saw the gull too and hissed and spat. That greedy gull! Well, Smokey meant to pounce on him if he possibly could. He saw Sooty up on the wall, watching. He would show him how brave he was!

Smokey's mistress came out with his dish of fish. How good it smelled!

"Smokey, Smokey!" she called. "Dinner! Where are you!"

Smokey stayed behind the dustbin waiting. His mistress went indoors.

As soon as she had disappeared, the big seagull glided down on outspread wings. It landed on the lawn and closed its wings, then walked quickly over to the dish, turning its back on Smokey. It was just about to peck up a large mouthful of fish when Smokey shot out from his hiding place, and pounced on the seagull's tail. He gripped it with claws and teeth, pulling with all his might.

The gull was very frightened. It gave a

loud cry, spread its wings and rose up
into the air – and what a sight to see – it
took poor Smokey with it!

You see, Smokey hadn't had time to
let go of the tail, and there he was, up in
the air with the gull, hanging on to the
tail-feathers for dear life!

Sooty watched with amazement. Now what would happen? Poor Smokey! Would he be taken right out to sea, and shaken off into the big waves?

The seagull was just as frightened as Smokey. It took a quick look round and saw that the heavy weight on its tail was a little black cat! It didn't know what to do! It couldn't peck him off in mid-air.

And then something most peculiar happened. The tail-feathers could no longer bear the weight of the cat – and they broke off! So, of course, poor Smokey fell from the seagull, the tail-feathers still in his mouth and claws,

and found himself falling, falling through the air. He was very frightened and Sooty, on the wall, miaowed in horror.

But, like all cats, Smokey landed on his feet. He found himself on the lawn, very shaken and surprised, but unhurt. He sat down to get his breath, his mouth full of white tail-feathers! Sooty called out to him.

"Smokey! Are you hurt? My – aren't you brave!"

Smokey spat out the tail-feathers, and looked proudly at Sooty. "Well – I won, didn't I? I've saved my dinner and pulled out the seagull's tail – though I didn't really mean to. I *was* surprised when he flew up into the air with me."

"Good old Smokey!" said Sooty. "I really must tell all the other cats about this. Come with me, Smokey. You'll be a hero!"

"No, I want my dinner before I'm a hero," said Smokey and ran to his dish. He gobbled up all the fish, and didn't even bother to keep a look-out for the seagull – no – he had defeated him for always! That gull would never dare come back.

Smokey was right. The big seagull kept well away from the gardens after that. Sooty and Smokey sat on the wall, looking up into the sky day after day – and how they miaowed when they saw the gull without a tail!

"There he is! Miaow-miaow! How strange he looks. We'll always know him now."

But they won't. The seagull's tail-feathers are already growing again, and soon he will look just like the others. What a shock he had that day when Smokey pounced on his tail – and what a hero Smokey is now!

Bunny's
First Christmas

"It's Christmas time!" said the big rocking-horse in the toyshop, one night when the shop was shut, and only the light of the streetlamp outside lit up the toys sitting on the shelves and counters.

"What's Christmas?" asked a small bear who had only just arrived.

"Oh, it's a lovely time for children," said the horse, rocking gently to and fro. "They have presents, you know, and Father Christmas comes on Christmas night and fills their stockings with all kinds of toys."

"You'll never fit into a stocking, Rocking-Horse!" said a cheeky monkey.

"No, I shall stand in somebody's playroom and give them rides," said the horse. "I shall look forward to that. I've been here a long time – too long. But I'm very expensive, you know, and people often haven't enough money to buy me."

"I should like to be sold and go to live with children who would love me and play with me," said a fat teddy bear. "I shall growl for them – listen – Urrrrrrr!"

"Don't!" said the little furry rabbit sitting next to him. "You frighten me when you do that. I think you're going to bite me."

"Don't worry. You know he wouldn't," said the clockwork sailor, leaning down from the shelf above. "Come on, Bunny – let's get down to the floor and have a game!"

The rabbit jumped down at once, and the clockwork sailor landed near him. He loved the sailor, who wouldn't let any of the bigger toys tease him or frighten him. Sometimes the pink cat chased him and the little rabbit couldn't bear that!

"Sailor," said the rabbit, when all the toys were playing together. "Sailor, we're friends, aren't we? Sailor, you won't leave me if you are sold and go to live with some children, will you?"

"Well – I shan't be able to help it," said Sailor. "You're my very best friend and I'm yours, and I hope and hope we'll be sold together – but you never know!"

The rabbit worried about that, and next day when customers came in and out of the shop, buying this toy and that, the little rabbit hoped that he and the clockwork sailor would be bought by the same person.

But they weren't! An old woman came in and asked for a sailor doll for her granddaughter whose father was a sailor and the shop lady at once took down the clockwork sailor from his shelf. "He's fine," said the little old woman. "Yes, I'll have him. My granddaughter Katy will love him! Will you wrap him up for me, please?"

"Goodbye, Sailor!" whispered the little rabbit, sadly. "Oh, I shall miss you so! Goodbye, and be happy!"

Sailor only had time to wave quickly while no one was looking. Then he was wrapped up in brown paper and carried out of the shop, leaving Bunny all by himself. Poor Bunny, he felt lonely and unhappy without his friend by his side. He hoped that the bear wouldn't growl at him or the pink cat chase him.

But that very day he was sold too! A nice, smiling woman came in and bought a great many toys at once.

"They're for a Christmas tree," she said. "I am giving a party on Boxing Day for my little girl and her friends, and

we've got a perfectly lovely tree to decorate."

"You'll want a pretty fairy doll for the top, then," said the shop lady, pleased. "And what about a little teddy bear and a doll or two?"

"Yes. And I'll have that toy ship – and that wooden engine – and that jack-in-the-box," said the customer. "And I really must have that little rabbit – he's sweet!"

Bunny was sold! He couldn't believe it. He was sold at last and would leave the toyshop he knew so well.

Bunny was very pleased to be going with so many other toys he knew. But, oh dear, each of the toys would be given to a different child at the party, so he wouldn't have any friends at all after Boxing Day!

The other toys were terribly excited. It was fun to be sold and leave the toyshop. It would be splendid to be part of the decorations on a beautiful Christmas tree and have crowds of children admiring them. And it would be simply lovely if they were lucky enough to be given to a

kind and loving child who would look after and play with them and perhaps even cuddle them in bed.

When they arrived at the smiling lady's house, Bunny was surprised to see such a big Christmas tree. It almost reached the ceiling!

"I don't think I want to be hung up there," he said to the fat teddy bear, who had been sold for the tree too. "I might fall off and hurt myself."

"Don't be such a coward," said the bear. "Ah – here comes someone to see to us! Cheer up, you silly little rabbit, and remember, if you are given to some horrid child, you must just run away and find a new home!"

"Run away? How?" asked the rabbit, anxiously. But the bear was very busy growling at that moment, because someone was pressing him in the middle where his growl was kept!

"Urrrr!" he said proudly. "Urrrr!" The little rabbit was hung high up on the tree, where he dangled to and fro. He didn't like it. The ground seemed so far away! All the other toys hung there too, and pretty fairylights shone brightly in red, blue, yellow and green from the top of the tree to the bottom.

"The party's tonight!" said a rag-doll next to him. "Not long to wait now! Doesn't the fairy look wonderful at the top of the tree?"

Soon the rabbit heard the sound of children's voices and laughter. They were playing games in another room. Then someone came into the big room where the tree stood and switched on all the fairylights again. The tree glowed and shone, and all the pretty ornaments on it glittered brightly. The toys looked lovely as they hung there.

How the children cheered and clapped when they came running in and saw the lovely tree.

"It's beautiful!" they shouted. "Oh, look at the toys! Can you see the fairy doll? Wave your wand, Fairy Doll, and do some magic!"

"Now, there is a toy for everyone," said the smiling lady who was giving the party. "Harry, here is a ship for you," and she gave him the toy ship. "Lucy,

here is a lovely rag-doll. I know you want one. Molly, I have just the toy for you – a bear with a growl in his tummy."

Soon there were only a few toys left on the tree. The little rabbit looked down on the children. Was there a little girl called Katy there? The sailor doll had been bought for a Katy. Oh, wouldn't it be wonderful if he was given to her, the same little girl who had the clockwork sailor?

Who was Bunny going to? He looked and looked at the children. He did hope that he would be given to somebody kind – a nice little girl, perhaps, with a merry face.

"And now, what about a present for you, Peter," said the kind lady. "You're not very old – I think you shall have this little furry bunny. Here you are!" So Bunny went to Peter, who held him very tight indeed, and squeezed him to see if he had a squeak inside. But he hadn't.

Bunny didn't like Peter very much, especially when he dropped him on the floor and somebody nearly trod on him.

"Be careful of your little rabbit, Peter," said a big girl.

"I don't like him," said Peter. "I wanted that wooden engine."

Poor little rabbit! He wondered if he could run away, just as the teddy had suggested. He didn't want to go home with Peter. He was sure he was one of the horrible children he had heard spoken about in the toyshop. But he did go home with Peter, and with him went a jigsaw puzzle for Peter's sister.

"Give this to your sister, Peter," said the kind lady. "It is such a pity she's in bed with a cold and can't come. This jigsaw shall be her present."

Peter carried the rabbit and the jigsaw home. As soon as he got there he went up to his sister's bedroom. She was in bed, with a large hanky under her pillow.

"Look – they sent you a jigsaw from the party," said Peter. "And all I got was this silly little rabbit!"

"Oh, Peter – he's sweet!" said the little girl in bed. "I've so many jigsaws – why

don't you take this one and I'll have the bunny instead. He shall come into bed with me. He looks rather lonely and, after all, he's only a baby one!"

"All right. I'd much rather have the jigsaw," said Peter. And he threw the rabbit to his sister and went out with the jigsaw underneath his arm.

Bunny landed with a thud on the bed, feeling very sorry for himself. Nothing seemed to be turning out as he had hoped.

The little girl picked him up gently and looked at him.

"Yes, I like you," she said, giving him a hug. "You shall sleep with me at night, so long as you don't mind sharing my bed with another toy. Look, here he is – my very best new toy!"

She pulled back the sheet – and Bunny stared in amazement. He couldn't believe his eyes. Who do you suppose was cuddled down in the bed, looking very happy? Why, it was Sailor!

Yes, it was the clockwork sailor doll, the one from the toyshop, Bunny's own special friend. Sailor almost sat up in surprise, but just in time he remembered not to. He smiled, though, he smiled and smiled! And so did Bunny!

"I think you like each other," said Katy, because that was her name, of course! "Yes, I'm sure you do. I hope so, anyway, because you've just got to be friends." And she gave both of them a happy hug.

"You see, you will sit together on my bed each day, and cuddle down with me at night," she explained, tucking Bunny in beside Sailor.

Katy kissed them both goodnight. Then she lay down, closed her eyes, and was soon fast asleep. And then – what a whispering there was beside her!

"You!" said Sailor, in delight. "What a bit of luck!"

"You!" said Bunny. "Oh, I can't believe it! What's Katy like?"

"Fine," said Sailor. "You'll love her. Oh, Bunny – what lovely times we're going to have! You'll like the other toys here, too, all except a rude monkey – but I won't let him tease you! Fancy, we shall

be able to be friends all our lives now!"

That was three years ago – and they are still with Katy, though they don't sleep with her at night now, because she thinks she's too big for that.

"It is nice to have a friend," Bunny keeps saying. Well, it is, isn't it?

Lightfeet and the Kite

Little Lightfeet, the pixie, leaned out of her window at the top of a tall tower. She did that every day, but however much she looked she could never see anyone riding along the winding road to the hill where the tower was built.

"If only there was someone I could wave to!" she thought sadly. "I've been a prisoner here for six weeks now, and nobody has been along to rescue me."

Lightfeet had been captured by a goblin. Her father was a rich fellow, and Spink hoped that perhaps when his little daughter had been missing a bit longer he would offer a fine reward for her.

"Then I should be rich!" thought Spink, rubbing his bony hands together. "Very rich. But I shan't let Lightfeet go unless her father pays many, many sacks of gold to me."

Nobody knew where little Lightfeet was. She had been taken away when she was walking by herself in the garden, looking at the purple and yellow crocuses that were blooming all over the grass nearby. Spink had come by, changed her into a crocus herself, put her in his buttonhole and walked off through the garden gates!

Nobody knew that he was wearing Lightfeet in his buttonhole! In fact, nobody really noticed the goblin at all.

He was able to take Lightfeet all the way to his tower, and there he changed her back to her own shape.

She was frightened and sad and lonely. She didn't like Spink at all. "Take me back home," she wept. "My father and mother will miss me."

Spink looked at the little pixie. She was very pretty. He didn't want to hurt her or make her unhappy, but he meant to keep her prisoner till her father offered a reward for her.

"Don't cry," he said. "I won't hurt you. I just want some money for you, that's all."

"You're mean and horrid!" wept Lightfeet. "Let me go!"

"No, not till I get paid for you," said Spink. "Your father is rich. He must pay me six sacks of gold."

"He hasn't as much as that!" cried Lightfeet. "Why, you would make him as poor as a church mouse if you asked him for even four sacks. You must be mad! I wouldn't let him pay all that for me. Oh, I don't like you. You are a nasty,

mean fellow. Go out of my sight!"

Spink went. He waited and waited
each day to hear if a reward had been
offered for Lightfeet. But none had. Her
father was sending messengers out
everywhere, asking for news of Lightfeet.
He was certain he would soon hear where
she was – and then he would send
soldiers to fetch her!

But not one of his messengers thought
of Spink the goblin, who lived so far away
in his tower on the hill. Nobody knew
much about him. So no one came riding
along the winding road to his tower, and

each day little Lightfeet looked out without seeing anyone except the peasant woman who sometimes brought eggs for Spink.

"You look pale," said Spink one day to the little pixie. "You didn't eat your breakfast today. Do you feel ill?"

"Of course I do!" said Lightfeet. "I'm used to the open air, and running about in a garden! Why can't I go down into your garden and play?"

"Well, I don't want anyone to see you," said Spink. "You know that."

"There's nobody to see me – and anyway, how could they?" said Lightfeet. "There's a very high wall all round the garden!"

Spink looked at Lightfeet. Certainly she had lost her rosy cheeks and bright eyes. Suppose she fell ill? He wouldn't dare get a doctor for her.

"Well," he said at last, "you can come down and play in the garden. But it's a very, very windy day, so you had better put on my old coat."

Lightfeet didn't want to wear the dirty

old coat, but the goblin buttoned it on firmly round her. Then he took the little pixie downstairs and out into the walled garden.

"Oh, how nice to be out-of-doors again," said Lightfeet. "How lovely to feel the wind and the sun! What shall I play at?"

"Well, when I was a goblin boy I used to fly a kite on a windy March day like this," said Spink, remembering. "Would you like to fly one? I've got my old one somewhere."

"Yes, I'd like to," said Lightfeet. "But have you got plenty of string? The kite

111

would fly nice and high on a windy day like this."

Spink went off to find the kite. Lightfeet put her hands into the pocket of Spink's old coat. She felt something in one of the pockets and took it out. It was a notebook with a pencil at the back.

"If only, only I could write a note and throw it over the wall!" she thought. "But nobody ever comes by! So what would be the use of that?"

Spink came out with the kite. It was a big one, but had no tail. He brought also a ball of strong string.

"Here you are," he said. "This kite used to fly well. I'll tie the string on for you, then you can fly it."

"I can do it myself, thank you," said Lightfeet, who couldn't bear the goblin near her. She undid some of the string and tied it to the kite.

She threw it up into the air. The wind took it, and it flew high – but almost at once it dipped and came downwards, dipped again, took a big swoop – and there it was on the ground!

"Bother!" said Lightfeet and tried again. But again the kite fell to the ground. Lightfeet looked all around. Spink was gone.

"This kite needs a tail made of paper twists," she said. "Then it would hold the kite properly and help it to fly. Where's Spink? I'll ask him for some paper."

But Spink had gone indoors. Then Lightfeet remembered the notebook. She would use the pages from that, twist them up, and tie them to an extra piece of string to make a tail for the kite!

She took out the notebook. The pages were all blank. She tore one out – and then she stopped.

"I've got an idea!" she whispered to herself. "A – very – good – idea! I'll scribble a message on these pages, twist them up to make a long tail, and then tie them to the kite. And I'll let the kite go! It will fly high up into the air and come down somewhere else far away. Perhaps – oh perhaps – someone will find it and read the message written on the paper tail!"

She took the notebook again, and got out the pencil from the back. She wrote one word on each of eight pages, then she tore them out and twisted each one to make a tail for the kite, tying them on to a piece of string one by one.

A voice shouted from the window. It was Spink leaning out angrily. "What are you doing? What are you using that paper for?"

"Only to make a tail for the kite," called back Lightfeet. "It won't fly. Surely you don't mind my doing that?"

"No. Make a tail if you like," shouted

Spink. "I remember now, it always flew better with one."

With trembling fingers Lightfeet fixed the tail on to the kite. Then she flung it up into the wind. The breeze caught it and up it went, high in the air. It flew marvellously now that it had a paper tail to balance it. Up it went, and up and up. Lightfeet let the string unwind until there was none left. She let the end slip right through her fingers!

The wind took the kite as high as the clouds. Lightfeet watched it. "Fly away, fly away," she whispered. "Fly to my friends with my message, Kite."

Then she pretended to wail and cry. "Oh, oh, the kite has gone! The wind took it away! Oh, oh, I've lost the kite!"

Spink was angry. He came running out at once. "What a thing to do!" he shouted. "We've lost it for ever! I was fond of that kite. Come indoors at once, you silly, stupid little pixie. Why did I ever let you out?"

The kite flew up and up into the sky. The wind had a fine game with it. Then the breeze dropped suddenly and the kite flew lower, waving its fine paper tail in the air. It dropped lower and lower – and then fell right into a field, miles and miles away from the garden where Lightfeet had first flown it.

A small brownie lived in the cottage nearby. He saw the kite fall, and ran out. He was a very young brownie, and he liked kites. He called his small sister, and they ran to the kite together.

"It's come to see us," said Peeko, the boy brownie. "Look at its fine tail, Bonnie. Some child must have made it for the kite."

Bonnie picked up the string and shook out the paper twists so that they hung straight. Her sharp little eyes suddenly saw a word written on the last twist of all.

"Oooh, look!" she said. "Lightfeet's name is written there – you know, Peeko, the little pixie who has been stolen away. Who wrote it there?"

"I don't know," said Peeko, astonished. "Look, there's a word on this twist, too – goblin, it says!"

"Oh, Peeko – could it be a message?" cried Bonnie. "Quick – let's undo all the twists and see what words are written on them."

They untied all the eight twists of paper and flattened them out. "Eight words," said Bonnie. "But all mixed up. We'll have to put them in their right order, Peeko. Look, here they are – Lightfeet, goblin, save, with, Spink, me, I, am. Eight words! Let's arrange them in the right order."

It took Peeko and Bonnie just four minutes.

"There you are," said Peeko, at last. "We've got a proper message now that the words are arranged in the right order! 'I am with goblin Spink; save me, Lightfeet.'"

"Fancy that!" said Bonnie, her eyes shining. "It's from little Lightfeet. That nasty old goblin Spink must have captured her. Let's go and tell someone."

Well, it wasn't long before everyone heard the news. Lightfeet's father was full of joy. He sent for twelve horse-soldiers, put himself at the head of them and rode off to the goblin's tower.

Clippety-clop, clippety-clop! Lightfeet heard them coming along the winding road, and leaned out of her window in excitement. *Clippety-clop!* Why, there was her father at the head of a glittering band of soldiers.

She shouted and waved – and down below, in his own room, Spink, too, saw the band of soldiers coming. He was afraid. Did they know Lightfeet was in his tower? No – they couldn't know.

Blam-blam! That was a thunderous knock on the door. Spink went to open it, afraid that the door would be broken in if he didn't go.

"We've come for Lightfeet – and for you too!" said the leading soldier, and caught Spink by the collar of his coat. "She's here all right, we know that. We got her message!"

And with that the other soldiers, with Lightfeet's father at the head, poured into the tower and up the stairs – and in a few minutes down they came again, with Lightfeet in her father's arms, crying and laughing at the same time!

Spink stared at little Lightfeet angrily. "How did you send a message?" he cried. "You couldn't have sent one!"

"Well, I did," said Lightfeet. "And I wrote it on the pages of your notebook, too, with your own pencil – I twisted up the torn-out pages and made a tail for the kite – and then I let the wind take it away. I was cleverer than you, Spink, wasn't I?"

"Don't talk to this wicked goblin," said her father, hugging her close. "We shall lock him up in his own tower, and see how he likes it!"

"And he won't be able to send a message out, because there isn't a kite now," said Lightfeet, laughing. "Goodbye, Spink – *you* won't be able to escape."

The Little
Wobbly Man

Jane had such a lot of toys, you might almost think her playroom was a toyshop!

There were dolls, bears, bunnies, dogs and everything else you can think of.

The prettiest toy of all was a fairy doll with glittering wings and curly golden hair. She was really lovely. She had come from the top of a Christmas tree, and Jane was very fond of her. So were all the toys, especially Sailor Doll and the big teddy bear.

There was a funny little plastic man in the toy-cupboard who had come from the same Christmas tree as the fairy doll. He had a heavy piece of lead at the bottom of his round body, so that when he was knocked over he sprang upright again at once and wobbled about. He couldn't lie down at all. He always stood upright. He loved the fairy doll very much, and she would have liked to be friends with him. But the sailor doll and the brown teddy bear jeered at him because he was only made of plastic, and so the fairy doll stayed away from him.

"What's he doing in our toy-cupboard?" the sailor doll said. "A creature made of hard plastic, instead of having proper clothes or fur! We won't have anything to do with him. He's a silly little wobbly man."

And they wouldn't speak to him – so he was very lonely and often wished that he was back on the big Christmas tree, hanging next to the wooden engine that he had liked so much.

Now one day a green goblin came to live in the tree outside the playroom window. He was a nasty little fellow with bright green eyes, green hair and a green suit. He had no wife and he was looking out for one – so when he looked in at the window and saw the pretty fairy doll, he fell in love with her at once.

"That's the wife for me!" he said to himself, his green eyes gleaming brightly. "She's as pretty as a fairy. No real fairy will marry me because I'm too bad-tempered, but I'll make the doll marry me. I'll carry her off!"

So he laid his plan carefully. He decided to creep in at the window one moonlit night when the toys were dancing together on the floor, and ask the fairy doll to dance with him. Then in the middle of the dance he would whisk her out of the window and that would be the last the toys ever heard of her!

But the little squirrel, who had overheard the green goblin talking to himself, warned the toys of what he was

going to do. So they planned that on the night when the goblin came, they would shut the window with a bang, and then he couldn't possibly take the fairy doll away. Then they would scare him away for good.

It all came about as they had planned. When they were dancing together to the tune played by the musical box, one bright moonlit night, the green goblin appeared at the window. He jumped down to the floor and went up to the fairy doll, who looked very frightened. The brown teddy bear at once shut the window so that the goblin could not escape with the doll – but the goblin didn't notice, for he was so eager to dance with the fairy doll that he didn't think of anything else at all.

The fairy doll shook her head.

"No," she said, firmly, "I don't want to dance with you. You are ugly."

With a cry of rage the green goblin snatched at her hand and dragged her to him. Then he tried to make her dance a few steps with him. She screamed and

struggled. The sailor doll rushed up and tried to take her away.

"I'll fight you if you don't give me the fairy doll," yelled the goblin, angrily. "I want her for my wife!"

"Let her go!" cried the sailor, in a temper. The goblin let go of the doll and rushed at the sailor doll. They began to fight – but after the goblin had hit him a few times the poor sailor began to be frightened, and puffed and panted as if he would burst. At last he fell down on the floor and couldn't get up. The goblin gave a cry of delight and rushed to get the fairy doll once more.

But this time the teddy bear pushed him away, and put up his big paws to fight. The goblin darted round and round the big clumsy bear, hitting him hard. The poor bear hadn't a chance, for he was slow and heavy. At last he fell down with a thud, hit his head against the wall and lay there in a faint. The goblin had won!

He rushed once more to get the frightened doll, and this time no toy dared to prevent him. The clockwork mouse, the stuffed animals and the jack-in-the-box were all afraid to move. The fairy doll screamed and tried to push the goblin away. "Oh help me, someone!" she cried. "Do help me!"

The little wobbly man quickly made up his mind. He was only made of plastic, but he wasn't going to see the fairy doll stolen away like that, even if the goblin battered him to bits. No, he was going to save her!

The goblin heard a funny rocking sound and saw the little wobbly man wobbling across the floor towards him. He laughed loudly. "Hello! Is this someone else coming to fight me? Poor little fellow, what use are you? You couldn't stand up to a mouse!"

"Yes, I could," answered the wobbly man, in a cool, calm voice. "Nobody can knock me down. Not even you, you nasty, horrid little creature!"

"How dare you call me names!"

shouted the goblin in a temper, and he rushed at the wobbly man and hit him hard. The wobbly man fell to the floor. But the heavy weight at the bottom of his body pulled him upright again, much to the goblin's surprise.

What a strange fight that was! No matter how hard the goblin hit him, the little wobbly man sprang upright at once, and soon the goblin became tired, and began to puff and pant. He wondered if

the little wobbly man had some magic about him that made him stand up every time he was knocked down. It really was most peculiar.

Poor little wobbly man! He was bruised and battered, but he kept springing back for more. *Bang!* The goblin smacked him on the head and down he went on the floor. Up he swung again, bashing into the goblin as he did so.

"You – can't – get – me – down!" panted the wobbly man. "You – can't!"

And the goblin couldn't! At last, quite worn out with trying, the goblin suddenly gave in. He shot up to the window, opened it and slipped out into the night – without the fairy doll! He was beaten by the little wobbly man who couldn't lie down!

What a hero he was! How everyone patted him on the back and praised him!

And you should have seen his face when the fairy doll slipped her arm round him and told him he was the bravest toy she had ever known, and, if he liked, she would marry him and live happily in the doll's-house with him ever after.

"Well, you know, I didn't really beat the goblin," he said, modestly. "It was just that I always have to swing upright as soon as I'm knocked down. I'm made that way, I can't help it!"

"You're a darling!" cried the fairy doll and kissed him on the cheek. He fell down flat with joy – but of course he sprang upright again immediately!

In the Heart of
the Wood

"Scamp! Scamp! Do you want to go for a walk?" shouted Billy. "Sally, are you coming too?"

A black Scottie dog flung himself on Billy and darted round in delight, his tail wagging hard. A walk! That was just what he loved!

Billy's sister came running downstairs. "Yes, I'm coming, Billy. Let's go to the wood and watch Scamp chasing the rabbits. They all have such fun. The rabbits know he can't catch them, but Scamp always hopes he will!"

So off went the three of them to the wood. Scamp tore in front, for he had heard the magic word "rabbits". Ah, one day he would catch one, he felt certain of it.

They came to the wood. It was a nice wood, but so deep and dark in the middle that the children had never walked right into the heart of it.

"Woof!" said Scamp, spying a rabbit cocking an ear at him behind a tree, and off he went. The rabbit tore off too, its white bobtail going up and down.

It went into a hole. "Scamp always thinks that's unfair!" said Sally, with a laugh. Scamp looked up at her. He thought that rabbits should live in holes that were big enough for dogs to get down!

Another rabbit flashed by. Off went Scamp, and this time he disappeared behind the trees. The children walked on after him. They walked for some time, and didn't see Scamp at all.

"We'll have to turn back soon," said Billy. "Scamp! Scamp! Come along now. Home, boy, home!"

Sally whistled. No Scamp came. Bother! Now they would have to look for him.

Into the wood they went, and then

heard, in the distance, Scamp's excited barks. But he took no notice of their calls. They hurried towards him, going deeper into the wood than ever before.

Scamp was chasing a rabbit round a tree – or was the rabbit chasing him? Sally laughed. The rabbit suddenly darted off, ran to the right, and disappeared at the foot of another tree.

But what a tree! The children stared in wonder at it. They had never seen a tree so big before. Scamp ran to it and sniffed about at the bottom, where there was a hole into which the rabbit had gone.

"Let's go and look at that enormous tree," said Sally. "My goodness – what a size it is round the trunk!"

Billy hit it hard, and then looked at Sally, his eyes shining. "It's hollow!" he said. "Let's climb up and look down into the hollow. Come on!"

So into the branches of the big tree they went, up and up. Then they looked down into the hollow. The heart of the trunk was empty and rotten – completely hollow. It was a wonder that the tree was still alive!

"Let's get down into the hollow, Sally," said Billy. "Do let's!"

Sally looked down into the tree. "But Billy," she said, "suppose we dropped down into the hollow and couldn't climb up again. We'd have to stay there for ever and ever. Nobody would hear our calls, you know."

"We'd better get a rope," said Billy, peering down into the vast empty heart of the tree. "Come on. Let's go back and

get it now. I feel excited! Why, the inside of that tree is almost big enough to play house in!"

They climbed down again and rushed home, Scamp following them. He felt rather pleased with himself, because it was he who had shown them the tree they thought so wonderful!

They found a long, strong rope in the garden shed, and went off with it again. Their mother called them back.

"You can't go off now," she said. "It's teatime."

"Oh well – we'll have tea and go afterwards," said Billy, who simply couldn't give up the idea of getting down into the hollow tree as soon as possible.

So after tea off they went. Billy had the rope tied round his waist. Scamp tore along in front, looking out for rabbits again.

"Here's the tree – gosh, it really is enormous!" said Billy, and he undid the rope round his waist. "Come on, Sally. Up the tree we go."

And up they went. They came to a good strong branch and Billy tied the rope firmly to it. Then he dropped the end down the middle of the tree. It fell into the dark hollow below.

"I wish we had a torch," said Sally, peering down. "There might be a rat down there, and I don't like rats."

"I've brought a torch, and there won't be rats," said Billy. "Anyway, Scamp will soon send them away if there are."

"You go first, Billy," said Sally. He swung himself down on the rope – down and down, hand over hand, his legs twisting together round the rope.

He dropped with a thud into the hollow of the tree. It smelled musty. "Come on, Sally," he yelled, feeling for his torch. "My word, it's like a small room inside this tree. It's most exciting."

Sally slid down the rope. She went too fast and her hands felt as if they were burning. She landed beside Billy, on to something soft. She wondered what it was.

"Do switch on your torch," she said. "Quick!"

Billy switched it on – and the light shone around them in the curious tree hollow. And then they noticed something very strange.

"Look," said Billy, puzzled, "what's that piled here and there? Sacks! Empty sacks! And look, here's an empty cardboard box! Sally – whatever are they doing here?"

"Somebody has been using this tree for something!" said Sally. "Oh Billy – whose tree is it? We'd better find out!"

"You know, Sally, I think someone is using this hollow tree to hide things in," said Billy. "Maybe a robber!"

"Gracious!" said Sally, scared. "Do you mean – a burglar, perhaps? There have been an awful lot of robberies lately, haven't there? And the police have never found any of the stolen goods."

"I say – I hope whoever uses this tree as a hiding-place doesn't come while we're here," said Billy, suddenly feeling uncomfortable.

"Well, Scamp is outside the tree. I can hear him snuffling round," said Sally. "He'd scare away any robbers!"

Scamp was scraping hard at a hole at the bottom of the hollow tree. Billy flashed his torch downwards and laughed. "Look – he's got his head inside the tree but he can't get his body through. Poor old Scamp! Mind you don't get stuck!"

"Let's look at these sacks and see if they tell us anything," said Sally. "There are so many of them – all empty too!"

"Wait a bit – here's one with something in!" said Billy, and he picked it up. He opened the neck of the sack and flashed his torch inside.

"Sally, look – what's gleaming inside there?" he said. "Pull it out."

Sally put in her hand and tugged. Out came a beautiful silver candlestick, with branching ends for candles. "Well!" said

Sally. "Look at that! This is a hiding-place for stolen goods!"

Scamp suddenly took his head out from the hole in the tree and began to bark loudly. Sally felt frightened.

"Billy! Scamp's barking," she said. "Do you think someone is coming? Oh I do hope it isn't the robbers!"

Scamp was barking his head off. "Woof, woof, woof! Woof, woof, woof! Grrrrr!"

"Look at that dog!" said a man's hoarse voice. "What's he doing there? Do you think there's anyone about in the woods this evening, Jim?"

"Might be," said another voice, rather low. "Dump the sack in that bush over there, Alf – where it won't be seen. Then we'll sit down with our backs to the hollow tree and wait a bit to see if the owner of the dog comes along. Maybe the dog's just rabbiting by himself."

Sally clutched Billy's hand as they heard this. Men with another sack! It must be the robbers! What would they say when they found the two children inside the tree!

142

"Shh!" said Billy, in Sally's ear. "Don't make a sound, Sally. Perhaps Scamp will send them off. Hear how he's barking."

The two men sat down with their backs against the tree. The children sat on the sacks, absolutely still. Scamp went on barking.

"He's just rabbiting," said one of the men at last. "Chuck a stone at him, Alf, and send him off!"

There was a piteous squeal from Scamp as a large stone struck him. Then the sound of scampering feet. "He's gone," said Alf. "Now to get to work!"

The two men got up. Billy felt Sally

trembling. How he wished their dog Scamp had not run away. Poor Scamp – he might have been badly hurt by the stone the man threw at him.

The men began to climb up the tree. The children could hear them quite plainly. Then one of them found the rope that Billy had tied to a branch, so that he and Sally could get down easily.

"Hey – look at this!" said one of the men. "Someone's been here! Our hiding-place has been found. Someone's been down in this hollow tree."

"Did we leave anything there in the sacks?" asked the other man. "Yes, we did – that silver candlestick we couldn't sell! Wonder if it was found. Alf, maybe a watch is being kept on this tree!"

"Yes, better get the candlestick quick and go," said Alf, and slithered down the rope!

He landed right on top of poor Billy. The boy gave a yell, and the man jumped in alarm.

"What's up?" called down the other man.

"Two kids here!" answered Alf, and he gave the children such a look that they shivered. "Two – silly – stupid – interfering kids! What are we going to do with them?"

"Ask them what they know," called down Jim. "Maybe no one else knows of this tree but them."

"We only found it a little while ago," began Sally, in a trembling voice. "Nobody else knows anything about it. Please let us go."

The men were very angry to think that their hiding-place had been found. Alf went up the tree and talked to Jim for a long time. Then he called to the children.

"Look out down there! There's a sack coming. Mind your heads!"

Billy pushed Sally aside. A sack came down and landed with a thud.

The children were astonished. Were the men going to go on using the tree then?

"We're coming back at midnight to fetch the things," called down Alf. "And you're going to stay down there in the tree, see, so that you can't go and tell anyone. If you're good children maybe we'll let you out then – if you're not we'll leave you down in the hollow!"

Sally gave a squeal. "Oh don't leave us here now. It's getting dark. Do let us go home. We won't say a word."

The men pulled up the rope that hung down into the hollow. Without that to help them up the children could not possibly get out of the tree. Whatever were they to do?

The men slithered down the tree and jumped to the ground. The children heard them going through the wood. Sally was very frightened.

"Oh, Billy – can't we get out? Will we have to stay here till midnight? What will Mummy say?"

"Cheer up. We'll have to stay," said Billy. "Curl up on the sacks, Sally. I'll look after you. I expect they'll set us free at midnight!"

The two children settled down on the sacks inside the tree. It was very dark now. Billy felt worried. He had always

been taught to look after his sister, and he didn't know how to put things right. How could they escape from the hollow tree when their rope was gone? It was quite impossible.

The children sat there in silence. Billy switched his torch on at times, just to cheer them up. He didn't like to leave it on all the time in case the battery wore out. He put his arm round Sally.

"Never mind, Sal," he said. "It's an adventure, you know!"

"Well, I don't like it," said Sally. "Oh, Billy, I hope those men really will come back. Suppose they left us here for ever?"

"Silly!" said Billy. "Of course they wouldn't." But all the same he felt very anxious too.

Suddenly there was a rustling sound outside the tree. Sally clutched at Billy's hand in fright. Whatever was it now? A robber creeping back? A rat? Oh dear!

"Scamp! It's old Scamp! Dear old dog, he's come back to find us!"

"Woof," said Scamp, cautiously, and stuck his head through the hole at the

bottom of the tree. He couldn't get any
further. He blinked up at them.

"Scamp, can't you rescue us?" said
Billy. "No, I don't see how you can. Look
at that place on his head, Sally – that
must have been where the robber's stone
hit him."

"Poor old boy," said Sally.

Suddenly Billy gave a cry and made
Sally jump. "Sally, Sally, I know what we
can do! We can write a note, and tie it to
Scamp's collar, and send him home with
it! Can't we?"

"Oh yes," said Sally, joyfully. "Of
course. Have you got a bit of paper, Billy.
I've got a pencil."

Billy wrote on the paper:

Mum, we are prisoners in a hollow tree in the wood. It's a hiding-place for stolen goods. The robbers came while we were in the tree and they have taken our rope so that we can't get out. They are coming back at midnight to get their goods. Please rescue us.

Scamp will show you where we are, if you follow him.

Love from Billy and Sally.

"Mum will be surprised to get a note like that," said Billy, and tied it firmly to Scamp's collar. He pushed it round so

it stood up plainly. Then he rubbed Scamp's nose. "Home, old boy," he said. "You go home with that note and find Mum. Home, old boy!"

Scamp was a clever dog. He understood. He pulled his head from the hole and backed away. Then the children heard his feet pattering through the wood.

"He's gone. Now we'll have to hope Mum sees the note and does something to save us," said Billy. "Cheer up, Sally. Things don't look so black after all!"

The wood was very dark and quiet, except when an owl hooted, or some small animal rustled here and there. The children sat and waited in silence, hidden deep inside the old hollow tree.

Billy looked at his watch.

"Oh dear – it's half-past eleven already," he said. "I wonder if Mum has found the note on Scamp's collar. Surely she would have been here by now if she had."

"Shh! I can hear something!" whispered Sally. "Oh – it's Scamp again, surely! And somebody with him!"

It was! The children heard his eager snuffling and then heard many footsteps. Quite a lot of people seemed to be following Scamp.

"Here's the tree," said their father's voice. "What an enormous one! Billy, Sally, are you there?"

"Oh yes, Daddy!" cried both the children. "We're still here. We thought you were never coming. Is Mummy there?"

"Yes," said their mother's anxious voice. "I've been so worried about you. Listen, we told the police about your note and they are here too, planning to catch the robbers. Have they been back again?"

"Not yet. They said midnight," said Billy. "Is that the police we can hear all around?"

"Yes," said a deep voice. "This is Inspector Jenks. We're going to get you out of that tree first, both of you. Then we're going to hide in the bushes around and completely surround the tree, to wait for the men to come back. We've got rope to haul you up. But we'll have to be quick about it!"

Someone climbed the tree, and soon after a rope came slithering down into the hollow. The children climbed out thankfully, dropped down the tree and ran to their parents. Scamp ran round and round, jumping up and down, he was so pleased to have them again!

"Now – you'd better get into the bushes too," said the inspector. "There's no time to take you back home. Not another sound please! Hold the dog, one of you children."

Then there was silence, while everybody waited. Scamp began to whine softly. That meant that someone was coming. Billy quietened him. "There's someone coming," he whispered to the inspector, who was close by him.

So there was! It was the two robbers coming back through the wood to the enormous hollow tree. They didn't know anyone was lying in wait. They didn't even lower their voices as they came!

They climbed the tree. They called down to the children who they thought were still in the tree. There was no answer, of course. Then down they jumped into the hollow – to find no one there!

The rest was easy. The police moved up and the tree was surrounded. The burglars were caught, their goods taken from them, and they were marched away to the police station!

"Oh, wasn't it exciting!" said Billy, as he and Sally and Scamp went home with their parents. "I did love it!"

"Too exciting!" said his mother. "Don't

do that sort of thing too often, Billy."

That wasn't quite the end of the story. The police sent Billy and Sally a lovely watch each for their help in catching the robbers – and Scamp had a beautiful blue collar with his name on it.

But he did deserve it, didn't he?

The Little
Ice-Cream Rabbit

Once upon a time Mr Two-Feet had a birthday party, and he ordered a grand ice-cream pudding for it. On the top was to stand a rabbit, all made of ice cream too. Oh, it was to be a wonderful pudding, I can tell you!

Mrs Biscuit, his cook, made the pudding, and she made the little rabbit too, to put on the top of it. It was a lovely little rabbit, in a pink ice-cream coat and brown chocolate ice-cream trousers. Mrs Biscuit was very proud of him.

But the rabbit didn't want to be on the ice-cream pudding. No, he knew he would be eaten, and he thought himself too grand for that. He wanted to go and play with the other rabbits out in the fields, and show them his wonderful coat and trousers. He knew that no other rabbit wore clothes, and he wanted to show off.

Mrs Biscuit left him on the cold windowsill, on top of the pudding. In a few minutes she would have to take the pudding into the dining-room, where Mr Two-Feet's party was going on. And the ice-cream rabbit took his chance to escape!

Yes, he jumped right off that ice-cream pudding, and ran out of the door. Mrs Biscuit saw him go and she called him back, very angrily.

"Rabbit, rabbit! Come back at once to your pudding! How dare you run away!"

But the rabbit only flicked his cold ears at her and ran all the faster. Out into

the backyard he went, and soon Mrs Biscuit saw him no more. How upset she was!

The ice-cream rabbit ran out of the gate. A little girl saw him and cried out in surprise.

"An ice-cream rabbit! Hey! Rabbit, rabbit! Come here to me! Don't run away!"

"You'd eat me!" cried the rabbit, and flicked his cold ears at her. The little girl ran after him, but he slipped under a hedge and she soon lost him.

The rabbit ran along the hedge, and suddenly a big brown cow saw him.

"Rabbit, rabbit!" she mooed. "Come here to me! Don't run away!"

"You'd eat me!" cried the rabbit and flicked his cold ears at the surprised cow. The big cow suddenly ran after him, but he scampered faster than ever, and the cow soon gave up the chase.

The ice-cream rabbit was out of breath. He sat down on a stone and took a rest. He was glad to be free.

"Ha, nobody will eat me now!" he said.

"I shall go to my cousins, the real rabbits, and live with them. They will be proud to have me."

Just then two long-eared rabbits popped their heads out of a hole nearby and looked hard at the ice-cream rabbit.

"Hello," said the ice-cream rabbit, grandly. "I've come to see you."

"What for?" asked the two rabbits.

"To show you my grand clothes," said the ice-cream rabbit, proudly.

"Well, we don't want to see them!" said the two rabbits, laughing. "We wear fur coats, and they are far better than your silly clothes. Fancy a rabbit wearing trousers! Ha-ha!"

The ice-cream rabbit was much offended.

"Oh, you don't want my company then?" he said, getting up and flicking his ears to and fro, and woffling his nose up and down. "Well, I'm sure I don't want yours! I wouldn't live with such bad-mannered rabbits as you for anything in the world!"

"Chase him, chase him!" suddenly cried the two rabbits, and to the ice-cream rabbit's great horror about twenty lively rabbits appeared and suddenly ran at him. He slipped through the hedge in

a second and ran across the road under a gate. The rabbits didn't dare follow him there, but they shouted rude things after him all the time. They certainly hadn't very good manners.

A cat was sitting by the gate, washing itself. When it saw the ice-cream rabbit it was very much surprised. It pounced after him.

"Rabbit, rabbit, come here!" it mewed. "Don't run away!"

"You'd eat me!" cried the ice-cream rabbit, and flicked his cold ears at the cat. He ran away as fast as he could, and went down the road again. Before he had gone very far two little boys saw him, and you can imagine how surprised they were!

"An ice-cream rabbit!" they cried. "Quick, get him!"

They ran after the frightened rabbit, shouting loudly.

"Rabbit, rabbit, come here! Don't run away!"

"You'd eat me!" cried the rabbit, and flicked his cold ears at them. He ran in at an open door, and hid behind a chair. The little boys didn't dare go in after him, and soon he felt safe. Then he heard a soft voice speaking to him.

"Little rabbit, what's the matter?"

The ice-cream rabbit turned round. He saw a big dog lying by the fire. At that moment the door slammed so the rabbit couldn't run away. He had to make the best of it.

"I'm an ice-cream rabbit off an ice-cream pudding," he said, nervously. "I've run away because I don't want to be eaten."

"Ice cream, are you?" said the dog. "Well, you must feel terribly cold, poor thing. Come near the fire."

The rabbit came nearer to the dog. Certainly the fire felt nice and warm.

"My word!" said the dog, opening his eyes wide. "You are a grand rabbit, aren't you! Pink coat and chocolate trousers and all! I've never seen a rabbit like you before!"

The rabbit was delighted. He woffled his nose and came nearer the fire.

"Yes," he said, "I'm a most unusual rabbit. All the field rabbits begged me to live with them, but I couldn't possibly live with such ill-mannered creatures, could I?"

This was a very naughty story, but the dog seemed to believe all the rabbit said.

"Of course you couldn't," he said. "Why, such a grand rabbit as you deserves to have the grandest of friends. Pray come nearer the fire and tell me all about yourself. I assure you I think it is a great honour to have your company."

The silly rabbit took the big dog at his word. He sat by the brick hearth and began to talk and talk, all about himself.

The big dog listened, and once or twice he licked his lips in a very strange way – just as if he were expecting a meal!

Suddenly the ice-cream rabbit felt rather strange and floppy.

"Excuse me!" he said, "I feel very sleepy. I must – just – take – a nap …"

His head nodded – and he began to melt! He was made of ice cream, you know, and of course he shouldn't have gone near a hot fire. It was very foolish of him.

Soon there was nothing left of him at all except an ice-cream puddle by the brick hearth. The dog got up and went to it. His red tongue went out and in rapidly as he licked up all that was left of the vain little rabbit.

"Grand! Grand!" said the dog – but whether he meant the rabbit himself, or the taste of him, nobody knows.

As for the ice-cream rabbit, when he woke up again, he wasn't there. Well, well, strange things do happen, don't they!

A Story of Tidiness and Untidiness

There were once two little girls called Julie and Jean. They were twins and did everything together.

One day their little brother caught chicken-pox, and Mother didn't want Julie and Jean to catch it too.

"I wonder who would have you to stay with them for a little while," she said. "You can't go to Aunt Kate's, she's away. I wonder if Great-Aunt Jane would have you?" Mother phoned to see. Great-Aunt Jane said she would have Julie and Jean, but they would have to make themselves useful around the house.

"Well, you two girls know how to dust and sweep and make your own beds," said Mother, "so you must just offer to do that for Great-Aunt Jane."

Off went Julie and Jean, rather excited to be going away to stay, and quite determined to do all they could to help their great-aunt.

Great-Aunt Jane lived in a dear little cottage, with a lovely garden full of flowers. She had two little puppies and a tiny kitten that played with them all day long. In the garden she had a little round pond with goldfish in it. Julie and Jean were very excited when they saw all these lovely things.

"Puppies and a kitten to play with!" said Julie.

"And a goldfish pond to sail boats on!" cried Jean. "What fun we'll have."

The next morning Great-Aunt Jane called them into her kitchen, where she was busy feeding the puppies and the kitten.

"I told Mother you would have to make yourselves useful around the house," she said, looking at them over the top of her big spectacles. "What can you be trusted to do? Girls don't work half as well nowadays as they used to in my young days."

"Great-Aunt, we will work well!" said Jean. "We can be trusted to do lots of things. We can dust and sweep and make our beds."

"Very well. Make your beds each morning. And Julie, you can dust the dining-room and sweep it and Jean can dust and sweep the sitting-room. Keep your own room tidy too. I'll come and watch you this morning. You'll have to work hard, you see."

Great-Aunt Jane chuckled at the twins. They laughed.

"Oh, that isn't much!" said Julie. "We shall soon get that done! Then we'll be able to play in the garden with the puppies, won't we?"

"Yes, you may," said Great-Aunt Jane. "But you must do your jobs thoroughly, do you understand? A job which is only half done is a disgrace to any girl or boy!"

Then she took them upstairs and watched them while they made their beds and tidied their room. Then downstairs they went and showed her how they dusted and swept.

"That's very nice, very nice indeed," said Great-Aunt Jane. "I hope you'll do it like that every morning."

The twins ran out into the garden.

"Isn't Great-Aunt particular?" said Julie. "It's an awful bother to dust in every corner like that."

"Well, Mummy's particular too," said Jean, who liked doing things well.

Julie didn't. She was an untidy little girl, and she usually left everything for Jean to do. But she couldn't at her great-aunt's because they each had different things to do.

The next day both little girls did their morning jobs. They straightened their sheets, plumped up the pillows, and made their beds beautifully. And each of them dusted and swept as carefully as could be. Then out they went to play with the puppies and to watch the goldfish as it swam.

But the next morning, Julie couldn't be bothered to dust properly.

"What does it matter if I leave the dark corners undusted!" she thought. "Nobody will see if I don't do them! And I do so want to go out into the garden and see what it can be that those puppies are squealing about!"

So out she went long before Jean, who was giving the sitting-room a very good dusting.

170

Next morning it was just the same. Julie didn't bother a bit about dusting in the corners. Nor did she on the next day, which was Saturday. She was out in the garden long before Jean.

But as Jean was dusting carefully behind a big saucer on the china cabinet, she came across a funny little flat parcel.

She picked it up. On it was written:

For Jean, with Great-Aunt's love. Buy a boat with this to sail on the goldfish pond.

Jean opened it. Inside was some money!

"Oh, how lovely!" cried Jean, rushing to thank Great-Aunt Jane. "What a good thing it was that I remembered to dust behind that saucer!"

She ran to show Julie. Julie was delighted to think they would have a boat to sail on the pond, but a little bit hurt because Aunt Jane hadn't given her some money, too. They bought a lovely boat and had a glorious time sailing it on the pond. Julie did so wish she had one as well.

The days went by and the little girls did their work every morning. Great-Aunt Jane never seemed to go and look how they were doing it, so Julie started to become more and more careless. She made her bed badly, and she didn't plump the pillows once. The next Saturday that came she bundled her bed together anyhow, and ran quickly downstairs to sail the boat before Jean came.

But Jean was a long time coming! She had made a lovely discovery. As she made

her bed she saw something long and flat lying beneath the pillows. She picked it up and undid the paper. It was a book of fairytales, with lots of pictures!

"How perfectly lovely!" cried Jean, and ran to thank Great-Aunt Jane again.

"I'm glad you like it," said Great-Aunt, smiling at her. "I know you must have made your bed properly, my dear, if you found that."

When Jean showed the book to Julie, Julie began to cry.

"Nasty old Great-Aunt Jane, to give you things and not me!" she sobbed. "Mum always gives us the same. Why doesn't Great-Aunt Jane?"

Just at that moment Great-Aunt came out.

"Dear, dear, dear!" she said. "What's all this to-do?"

"Julie's crying because you didn't give anything to her," said Jean. "Why didn't you, Great-Aunt?"

"Oh, but I did!" said Great-Aunt Jane. "Come and see."

She took the two little girls into the dining-room which Julie was supposed to dust each morning.

"Did you dust behind the clock on the mantelpiece?" she asked Julie.

Julie went very red. She knew there were lots of corners in the room she had missed.

"No," she said, "I didn't."

"There now!" said Aunt Jane. "And I put some money for you there last Saturday, because I wanted to pay you for dusting so nicely. Well, well. I must have it back, as you didn't dust properly. See if it's there."

Julie peeped behind the clock. Yes, there was a little flat parcel with *Julie* written on it. And wasn't it dusty!

Great-Aunt Jane solemnly undid the parcel and put the money back into her purse. Then she took them upstairs to their bedroom.

"Did you plump your pillows this morning?" she asked Julie.

Julie hung her head and said no, she hadn't.

"Dear, dear, dear!" said Great-Aunt Jane. "Then I suppose your fairytale book is still under the pillows! Why don't you take a look and see!"

It was! And very sadly Julie watched her great aunt put it away in a cupboard.

She was terribly ashamed and made up her mind never ever to do her work carelessly again.

"You are going home today," said Great-Aunt Jane, "and you may each take a puppy for your own, because I have enjoyed having you. Jean, go on doing your jobs well, and you will be a great help to your mother. Julie, don't forget the lesson you have learned while you have been here with me!"

And the funny old lady smiled at them so kindly that Julie smiled back through her tears and thought what a silly girl she had been.

Then the twins went upstairs, packed up all their things in their bags, tucked their puppies under their arms, and went downstairs again to say goodbye to Great-Aunt Jane.

When Julie said goodbye to her great-aunt, she kissed her and whispered something into her ear.

"I'm sorry I worked so very badly," she said, "but I promise I never will again."

Great-Aunt waved goodbye to them as

176

they went off. The twins were sorry to leave the dear little cottage, but they were most excited to be going home to their parents again.

"Whatever do you think Mummy will say when she sees our puppies?" said Jean.

Mother was delighted to have her two little girls home again, and Great-Aunt Jane had already asked her if the twins might have the puppies. She wondered why Jean had a ship and a book as well, while Julie had none, but she asked no questions.

But she was surprised to find, after only a few days, that instead of one very tidy little girl and one very untidy little girl, she had two of the tidiest little daughters you can imagine.

She couldn't make it out. Julie's bed was always as well made as Jean's, and instead of hurry-scurrying over it, and getting everything done first, she found that Julie was often longer than Jean.

"Well, really!" said Mother to Father one night. "I honestly don't believe any mother has got two such thorough little girls as we have. I really don't think you'd be able to find a single speck of dust anywhere in the house, no matter how hard you looked!"

Julie and Jean were very pleased to hear that, and Julie was delighted when Mother said she really must phone Great-Aunt Jane and tell her how helpful the twins were.

Two days afterwards there came a great *rat-tat-tat* at the door. Mother opened it, and took a big, exciting-looking parcel from the postman.

"Why, it's addressed to Julie!" she said.
Julie was most excited. She undid the
string and opened the parcel.

Inside was a lovely fairytale book!
There was a letter too, and when Julie
opened it, some money fell out!

Dear Julie, wrote Great-Aunt Jane.
"I think these belong to you now, don't they? If you buy a ship like Jean's, do please come and stay with me again and sail it on my pond. Don't forget to come soon, will you?

Wasn't that nice of Great-Aunt Jane?

The
Unhappy Teddy

In Jack's playroom there was a toy-cupboard. In it lived a happy family of dolls, bunnies, soldiers, a panda, a teddy bear, a pink cat, a lamb, a clockwork train, and a box of bricks. Jack played with them each day, and he loved them all very much.

One day a little boy called Peter came to tea with Jack. After tea they decided to play some games. Jack brought out all his toys and told Peter that he could play with any he liked.

But the toys soon found that Peter was not as gentle with them as Jack. Peter threw the dolls into a heap, broke one of the toy soldiers, and twisted off the lamb's tail.

"Be careful, please," said Jack, politely.

"Toys don't like being hurt, you know."

"They don't mind!" said Peter, picking up the pink cat. He began to play ball with the pink cat, throwing it up and down in the air. The pink cat hated it and began to feel very sick.

When it was time for Peter to go home, he caught sight of the teddy bear, and picked him up.

"Give me this," he said to Jack.

"You mustn't ask for things like that," said Peter's mother.

"I want it," said Peter. "Give it to me, Jack."

Now Jack loved Teddy, and he didn't want to let Peter have him. He felt certain that Peter would treat Teddy badly. So he didn't say anything.

"Now be a kind little boy," said Jack's mother. "You have lots of toys, Jack. Surely you can spare old Teddy for Peter."

So Jack had to let Peter have the teddy bear though he was very sad indeed to part with him. Peter went off holding the teddy by one leg.

The toys were very upset. They were all very fond of Teddy, and it was sad to think of him living with a rough little boy like Peter. They waited until Jack had gone to bed, and then they held a meeting about it.

"We must do something to help Teddy," said the curly-haired doll.

Just as they were all talking, they heard a tap-tap-tap on the window, and looked up. On the sill sat the little robin that Jack fed every morning.

"I say!" said the robin. "I've just come from Peter's room. He's got Teddy!"

"Yes, we know," said the toys, sadly.

"Is Peter treating him well?"

"No," said the robin. "Teddy's very unhappy. Peter has torn his coat off and he's lost one of his shoes. Now he's standing on his head in the corner and Peter has left him there and gone to bed. Teddy says he thinks he'll be really ill if he has to stand upside down any longer. So he has sent me to ask you if you can rescue him."

All the toys began to talk together excitedly. They were very angry and felt sorry for poor Teddy. But how could they rescue him? None of them could walk as far as Peter's house, and the robin was too small to carry them on his back.

Then the clockwork train spoke in a loud, puffing voice.

"If one of you could wind me up, I think I could go and fetch Teddy," he said.

The toys cheered in delight. They thought it was a splendid idea.

"But you won't last till you get to Peter's," said the panda. "Your clockwork will run down."

184

"Then one of you must come with me to wind me up when I run down," said the clockwork train. "Somebody must drive me too, for I can't see very well, you know."

"I'll drive you," said the rag-doll, climbing into the cab of the train.

"And I'll come with you to wind you up," said the panda. So it was all settled.

"Is Peter's playroom on the ground floor like Jack's?" asked the rag-doll.

"No," said the robin. "It's upstairs. Can the train climb the stairs?"

"No, I can't," said the engine.

"You'd better fly off and tell Teddy to walk down the stairs and stand at the front gate if he can. We'll pick him up there," said the panda.

So the robin flew off. As soon as the robin had left, the panda wound up the engine. It chugged across the floor, out of the door and down the passage. Luckily, the side door stood open and no one was about. The little engine chugged out of the door and down the path to the gate. Through the gate they went and out into the road.

"The robin said we turn left here," said the panda. "And then right at the bottom of the road."

"Fine," said the rag-doll. "Clockwork train is easy to drive."

The little engine puffed along the street but halfway along it began to slow down, then it stopped. Its clockwork engine had run down.

The panda hopped out of the cab and wound it up again. Off the little train went once more. An old woman who caught sight of it thought it was a big mouse and ran home in fright to tell her husband. The panda had to wind the engine up three times before it arrived at Peter's front gate.

The Unhappy Teddy

The robin had given Teddy the message. But how could he get downstairs when he was stuck on his head in a corner! Teddy shook his head sadly and a large tear rolled down his face.

"I can't move," he sighed. "My feet can't reach the ground."

"Don't cry," said a big rag-doll. "I'll help you."

"So will I," said a tall wooden soldier.

"We'll soon have you on your feet again."
Together they lifted poor Teddy up and
set him on his feet.

"Oh, I can't thank you enough," said
Teddy. "Now I can go home to Jack. I'm
sure he's missing me."

Teddy crept to the playroom door and
peeked out. There was no one around.
He turned and waved goodbye to the
toys.

"Thank you," he whispered and
slipped out of the door.

He tiptoed down the stairs into the
hall. The front door was shut, but a
window in the dining-room was still

open. Making not the slightest sound, Teddy climbed out of the window and ran quietly down the path to the gate. He and the robin waited together in excitement, longing to see the clockwork train coming down the road.

At last it came. Teddy hugged the panda and the rag-doll in delight.

"It is good of you to rescue me!" he said. "I have been so unhappy."

"Come on," puffed the engine. "Wind me up again, Panda, for I'm nearly run down. Let's go back home before it gets too dark."

"Look out," cried Teddy. "Here comes a policeman!"

Panda quickly wound up the clockwork engine and jumped back into the carriage. Then off they started again. The policeman saw them and stopped in amazement. But the little engine ran right between the policeman's legs and Teddy, the panda and the doll waved their hands to him as they went by.

The policeman simply couldn't believe his eyes! He stared after them in

astonishment as they puffed away down the street.

Panda had to wind the engine up three times before it reached Jack's house. It slowly chugged up the passage to the playroom. Then it stopped, panting, and all the toys crowded round in joy.

"Teddy's safe, Teddy's safe!" they cried, and they hugged and kissed one another. Teddy threw his arms round the brave engine and hugged it too.

Then the toys all said goodnight to the robin and climbed into the toy-cupboard. They were all so tired that they fell fast asleep within seconds.

How surprised Jack was in the morning when he opened the toy-cupboard to find his teddy sitting on the shelf.

"Why, I gave you to Peter!" he cried, picking Teddy up and giving him a hug. "However did you get back, Teddy? What a lovely surprise! Well, I shan't tell anyone, for I don't want to have to send you back to that little boy again!"

So he kept the secret. Nobody ever knew that Teddy had come back except Jack himself and the other toys, of course.

As for Peter, he hunted all over the house for Teddy, and he couldn't think where he had gone to! The robin on the windowsill could have told him – but you may be quite sure that it didn't!

Star Reads Series 2

Enid Blyton

Magical and mischievous tales from Fairyland and beyond....

The Wonderful Torch

...and other stories

978-0-75372-653-2

The Flopperty Bird

...and other stories

978-0-75372-652-5

The Fairy Kitten

...and other stories

978-0-75372-642-6

The Enchanted Shoes

...and other stories

978-0-75372-651-8

Peronel's Magic Polish

...and other stories

978-0-75372-650-1

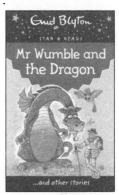

Mr Wumble and the Dragon

...and other stories

978-0-75372-649-5